Books by Hanna Kraan

TALES OF THE WICKED WITCH

THE WICKED WITCH IS AT IT AGAIN

FLOWERS FOR THE WICKED WITCH

FLOWERS
FOR THE
WICKED WITCH

HANNA KRAAN

with drawings by
ANNEMARIE VAN HAERINGEN

translated by
WANDA BOEKE

FRONT STREET 8 LEMNISCAAT
Asheville, North Carolina
1998

Copyright © 1994 Lemniscaat b.v. Rotterdam
English translation copyright © 1998 by Wanda Boeke
Originally published in the Netherlands under the title
Bloemen voor de boze heks
All rights reserved
Printed in the United States of America
First edition, 1998

Library of Congress Cataloging-in-Publication Data

Kraan, Hanna
[Bloemen voor de boze heks. English]
Flowers for the Wicked Witch / Hanna Kraan
with drawings by Annemarie van Haeringen; translated by Wanda Boeke.
—1st ed.
p.   cm.
Summary: The continuing adventures of a not-quite-so wicked witch who
lives in the forest with an owl, a hare, and a hedgehog.
ISBN 1-886910-35-9 (hc)
[1. Witches – Fiction. 2. Forest Animals – Fiction]
I. Haeringen, Annemarie van, ill. II. Boeke, Wanda. III. Title.
PZ7.K857F1 1988
[Fic] – dc21   98-41296

CONTENTS

FLOWERS
FOR THE
WICKED WITCH

WHISPERING WEED

Early one morning the hare and the hedgehog were walking through the forest.

"How beautiful everything looks," said the hare with satisfaction. "We do live in a good forest, don't we?"

"Too bad a witch lives in it, too," said the hedgehog, yawning.

"The witch isn't as bad as all that. Sometimes she's a little bothersome, but . . ."

The hedgehog stopped in his tracks. "There she is! Let's go back."

"Why?"

"It's still too early to run into a witch," the hedgehog explained. "I have to be wide awake for that."

"She's not coming this way at all," said the hare. "She's walking away."

"There she is again," said the hedgehog. "She *is* coming this way."

"Now she's turning around again," said the hare. "That's funny. She keeps walking back and forth in that tall grass. Do you think she's looking for something?"

"That grass . . . ," said the hedgehog, "I've never seen it there before."

"Now that you mention it, I haven't either. Maybe it just came up."

"It's strange grass," said the hedgehog. "And the witch is acting strange, too."

The witch walked, smiling and nodding, back and forth among the tall grass stalks. Finally she turned around and shuffled away.

"There she goes," said the hare.

"It's about time," grumbled the hedgehog.

"And now I want to know what she was doing there," said the hare. "Come on."

Together they ran down the path.

"What strange grass," said the hare. "I've never seen such thin blades. Have you?"

"Me neither."

"Stupid hedgehog!" came a whisper.

"Hey!" said the hedgehog indignantly. "Are you talking to me?"

"I didn't say that," said the hare. "Somebody else did."

"Strange hare!" came a whisper.

"Did you say that?" asked the hare.

"No, honest, I didn't. I didn't say anything."

The hare looked around. "Is somebody there?"

"You can hear a sound, but see nothing around," came the whisper again.

"Somebody's in the grass," said the hedgehog.

The hare went to look. "I don't see anybody."

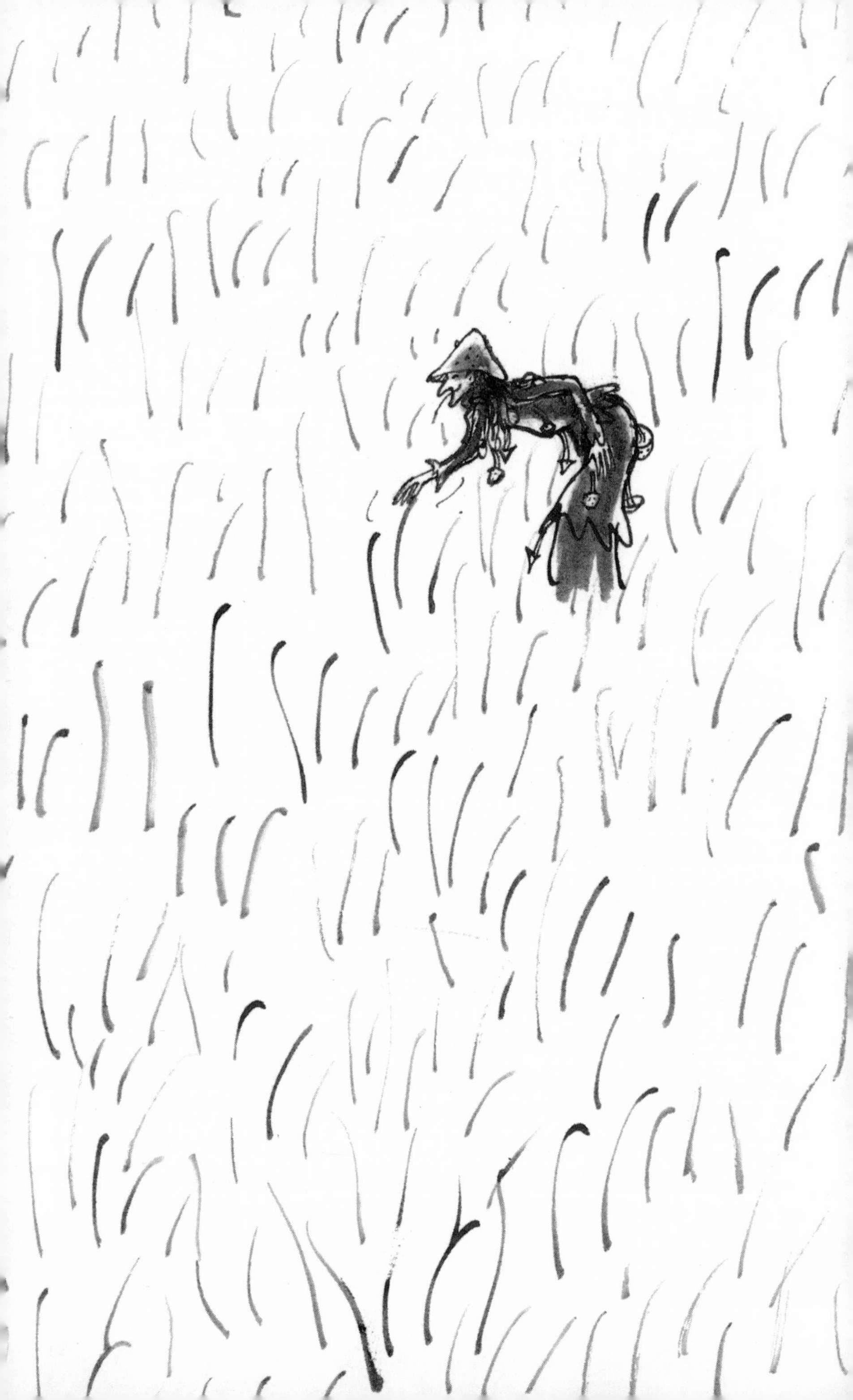

"A little somebody," said the hedgehog. "An ant or something."

"Not ants or any plants, we're the ones whispering."

"I think it's creepy," squeaked the hedgehog. "I want to go home." And he started to run away.

"Stupid hedgehog, stubbly ledgelog! The hedgehog is scared!"

The hedgehog came back. "I am not scared! Stop that whispering and come out. Then you'll see who's scared."

There was the sound of quiet giggling.

"That's odd," said the hare. "It seems as if the grass is whispering."

"How can that be?" said the hedgehog. "Grass can't talk, can it?"

"Try to listen closely."

"One and all we tease, we are whispering weeds."

"Whispering weeds!" said the hedgehog. "Something new again. I've never heard of that."

"Me neither," said the hare. "But I think the witch knows more about this." He looked up. "Ah, there's the owl."

The owl came walking up slowly. He was looking at the ground and mumbling:

*"Snow falls through the sky
with a cold sigh."*

"Owl!" the hare called out. "Listen to this. Something funny's going on around here."

*"Snow falls through the sky
with a gentle sigh."*

"He's thinking up poems again," said the hedgehog. "So he won't hear anything." He tugged at the owl's wing. "There's whispering here!" he shouted. "Coming from those blades of grass."

"Sure, sure," said the owl absently. *"White flakes . . ."*

". . . make frightful cakes," whispered the grass.

The owl started and glanced up in surprise at the hare. "Frightful cakes? What do you mean?"

The hare patted him on the shoulder. "We didn't say that. The grass did."

"The grass?" The owl stared anxiously at the blades of grass. "But, but . . . that's impossible, isn't it?"

"Everything's possible and the owl is scared. Just like the hedgehog," hissed the grass.

"I am not scared!" yelled the hedgehog.

"I'm not either," said the owl hesitantly. "But this isn't how it's supposed to be. This . . ."

"Are you all having an argument?" asked a shrill voice.

The animals looked around. The wicked witch was standing on the path.

The hare pointed at the grass. "That grass can talk. It's whispering at us."

The witch chuckled. "This is whispering weed. When you walk by, it whispers."

"Did you do that with magic, ma'am?" asked the hare.

"Of course!" said the witch proudly. "It was a lot of work, I'll tell you that. But I managed."

"Those blades of grass are calling me names," the hedgehog complained. "They don't have any manners."

"They do have manners, heeheehee," tittered the witch. "Just listen." She walked slowly past the grass.

"The smartest witch in the world," the grass whispered. "She does magic as nobody else can. Nobody knows as much as she does. She can cast any spell she wants. Clever witch."

The witch walked back and forth smiling, nodding her approval.

"You heard it," she said over her shoulder. "They do have manners."

And she walked on, humming to herself.

The animals looked at one another.

"No wonder she likes to walk here," said the hare.

"But *I* don't like to walk here," said the hedgehog. "I don't like it, being called names."

"I don't either," said the owl. "But I can just fly over it."

"*You* can! But *we* have to put up with that sneaky whispering."

Deep in thought, the hare stared at the whispering weed. "Maybe I have an answer," he said. He thought for a moment longer, then he nodded. "Yes, that's the way we'll do it. We'll hide in the grass. Make yourselves as small as possible, or else the witch will see us."

"And then what?" asked the hedgehog.

"Then we'll whisper, too! Things she won't think

are so nice to hear." The hare glanced down the path. "Here she is again. She just can't get enough. Quick!"

The animals hid themselves in the grass.

There was the witch, shuffling up. Near the whispering weed she slowed down.

"The best witch in the world," whispered the grass. The witch nodded.

"The stupidest witch in the world," whispered the hare.

"She can't cast spells well at all," whispered the owl.

"She just makes believe," whispered the hedgehog.

The witch stood still. "What's going on?" she muttered. She walked on warily.

"Clever witch," murmured the grass.

"A nix of a witch," hissed the hedgehog.

"She thinks she can do everything, but it isn't true," whispered the owl.

"She's better off cooking up magic potions," whispered the hare. "They don't talk back."

The witch had become very pale. "Watch out, whispering weed!" she cried. "Ooyooyooy!"

"Nobody's as smart as she is," the grass rustled.

But the hare quickly whispered, "At least that's what she thinks."

The witch took a deep breath. Then she pointed at the whispering weed and snapped, "That's enough out of you! Rude grass stalks! I'll turn you all into blueberries!"

Immediately the whispering weed disappeared and blueberry bushes appeared.

The witch stomped off home.

The animals came out from behind the berry bushes and watched her go.

"Sometimes she does have good ideas," said the hedgehog as he stuffed a handful of blueberries into his mouth.

THE TENT

"It's good weather for a walk," said the hare. He walked to the tree where the owl lived and looked up.

The owl was sitting on a branch, mumbling:

"Leaves flutter and branches creak,
apple pie would be a real treat . . ."

"Owl!" the hare called up. "Want to take a walk with me?"

The owl started and glanced down. "Walk? Where to?"

"To the pond."

"Good, I'll go. Do you want to hear my poem first?"

"Let's first walk to the pond," said the hare.

The owl flew down. "Then I'll let you hear my poem there."

Together they walked down the path. When they reached the clearing in the middle of the forest, they stopped.

"Well, look at that," said the hare. "A tent!"

In the middle of the clearing stood a tent made of an old curtain. The hedgehog stood in front of the entrance, pulling on the cloth to smooth it.

"Hedgehog!" the hare and the owl called out. "Is that your tent?"

The hedgehog jumped in fright. "Mercy!"

"Don't be frightened," said the hare. "It's just us."

The hedgehog turned around. "I didn't hear you two coming."

"What a beautiful tent," said the owl as he sauntered over. "How does it stay up?"

"Oh, you know. With a pole and a couple of branches."

The owl peeked in. "You did a good job."

The hedgehog nodded proudly.

"How did you come by that nice straight pole?" asked the hare.

"Found it," said the hedgehog. "What are you two doing?"

"Taking a walk. To the pond. You want to come?"

"Which way are you taking to the pond?"

"That way," said the hare, pointing.

"But then you pass the wicked witch's cabin."

"So? That doesn't matter, does it?"

"No, no, of course not," said the hedgehog. "But I still have to do something to my tent. I'll stay here."

"Then we'll come by later," said the hare. "We can have a rest in the tent."

"And I'll recite my poem," the owl promised.

The hare and the owl walked on. They passed by the witch's cabin.

"Maybe the witch will want to hear my poem," said the owl.

"We can always take a peek to see if she's home," said the hare.

"Ooyooyooy!" resounded from the cabin. "Ooyooyooy!"

"She's home . . . ," said the owl, looking pale.

The door flew open and the witch stormed out. "My broom! Where is my broom!"

"Your what, ma'am?" inquired the owl.

"My broom's gone! Did you two steal it?"

"No, of course not," said the hare. "Why would we?"

"Surely you just haven't looked well," said the owl.

"I did look well! Out of my way, or I'll change you two into a horsefly, a silverfish, a weevil, a . . ."

"Get out of her way!" cried the owl hoarsely and he flapped into a tree.

The hare dove behind a bush.

"Who has my broom?" the witch ranted. "Stop that thief!"

She disappeared among the trees, stamping her feet.

The hare came out from behind the bush and wiped his forehead. "Phew!"

The owl flew down. "She isn't in the mood for a poem," he said with a sigh. "Too bad. What do we do now?"

"Hm," said the hare. "The pond is that way and

that's where the wicked witch is. I think we'd better not take a walk there today."

"Then we'll do it another time," said the owl. "Let's go back to the tent."

They walked back to the clearing. The hedgehog lay sprawled in front of his tent. "Are you two back already?"

"Yes," said the hare. "We can't go to the pond because the witch is there, tearing around in a rage."

"Somebody stole her broom," explained the owl.

"Is that so?" said the hedgehog, yawning.

The hare rubbed his chin in thought. "Now who could have done that?"

"I'm sure she didn't look for it very well," said the owl. He stared down the length of the path. "As long as she doesn't come here . . ."

"We'll just go sit in the tent," said the hedgehog. "Then she won't see us."

He crawled inside and the others crawled in behind him.

"You see how big my tent is?" asked the hedgehog. "We can all fit."

The owl looked up anxiously. "As long as it doesn't fall down."

"Oh, it won't," said the hedgehog and he tapped the pole in the middle. "It's sturdy."

"A nice sturdy pole," said the hare, nodding. He took another good look. "That pole looks familiar to me. Where have I seen it before?"

The hedgehog coughed and nudged the owl. "You

had a poem, didn't you?"

"Yes!" said the owl happily. "I'd almost forgotten. How did it start again? Oh, right: *Leaves flutter and branches creak, apple—*"

"Wait a minute!" cried the hare. "Now I see it. That pole! That's the wicked witch's broom!"

"The br-br-broom," stammered the owl. "Take it away! Back it goes! Any second the witch will be here and then . . ."

All at once the tent was yanked away and there stood the wicked witch.

"Aha! There's my broom!"

The hedgehog jumped to his feet. "Just what do you think you're doing!" he shouted. "My tent! All gone!"

The witch pulled the broom out of the ground and slowly stepped toward the hedgehog. "*Your* tent! So *you* stole my broom!"

The hedgehog took a step backward. "Not stole. Borrowed! I was going to bring it back tonight."

"Oh, sure! You thief! Broom thug! I'll turn you into a weevil!"

"You should have just asked," said the hare.

"Asked!" said the hedgehog with a sneer. "She'd have just said no."

"Of course I'd have said no. I don't lend out my broom."

"But I needed a straight pole. Otherwise the tent wouldn't stay up."

"You call that a tent?" jeered the witch. "A broom

with an old curtain thrown over it?"

"It was a nice tent," said the hedgehog with a sniff. "We could all fit. And now you've gone and ruined it."

"We'll help you set up a new one," said the hare. "With a sturdy stick from the forest."

"But first I'm going to turn you into a weevil," said the witch and she took a step closer.

"Help!" squeaked the hedgehog.

"Whoa!" said the hare, standing in front of the hedgehog.

"Step aside," growled the witch, "or I'll turn you into a weevil, too."

The hare took a deep breath. "But everything's all right, isn't it, ma'am? You have your broom and the hedgehog will never borrow it again."

"Never again," whispered the hedgehog.

The witch wanted to say something, but the hare continued, "And now you must be quiet for a moment because the owl has made a poem especially for you."

The witch looked at the owl in surprise. "Especially for me?"

"Uh . . . yes," said the owl. "Especially!" He cleared his throat and said solemnly,

"Leaves flutter and branches creak,
apple pie would be a real treat.
All the . . ."

"Apple pie!" said the hedgehog. He swallowed. "I sure would like some."

"Shhh!" the witch hissed.

"But we can listen better if we have something to eat while we listen. Can't you conjure up an apple pie?"

"I can, but I'm not going to," snapped the witch. "Shouldn't have stolen my broom."

"You see how she always says no?" the hedgehog said to the hare.

"*All the paths* . . . ," the owl said pointedly and he looked sternly at the hedgehog. "*All the paths* . . ." He stopped.

"And?" asked the witch. "How does it go?"

"I don't know anymore," the owl said unhappily. "You're all talking through it and now it's gone."

"What a shame," said the witch in disappointment.

"It'll come back to you," said the hare. "It'll pop into your head again in no time."

"After you've had some apple pie," said the hedgehog. Full of hope, he looked at the witch.

"Maybe that would help . . . ," said the owl.

"Apple pie is good for the memory," said the hare. "That's a known fact."

"Really?" asked the witch. She mumbled something and—*poof!*—there was an apple pie on the ground.

"Hurrah!" the animals cheered.

The witch gave everyone a piece of pie and then looked at the owl with anticipation. "Is it helping already?"

"Mmm," said the owl with his mouth full. "It's starting to come back just a little." He glanced at the pie from the corner of his eye. "But not all the way yet."

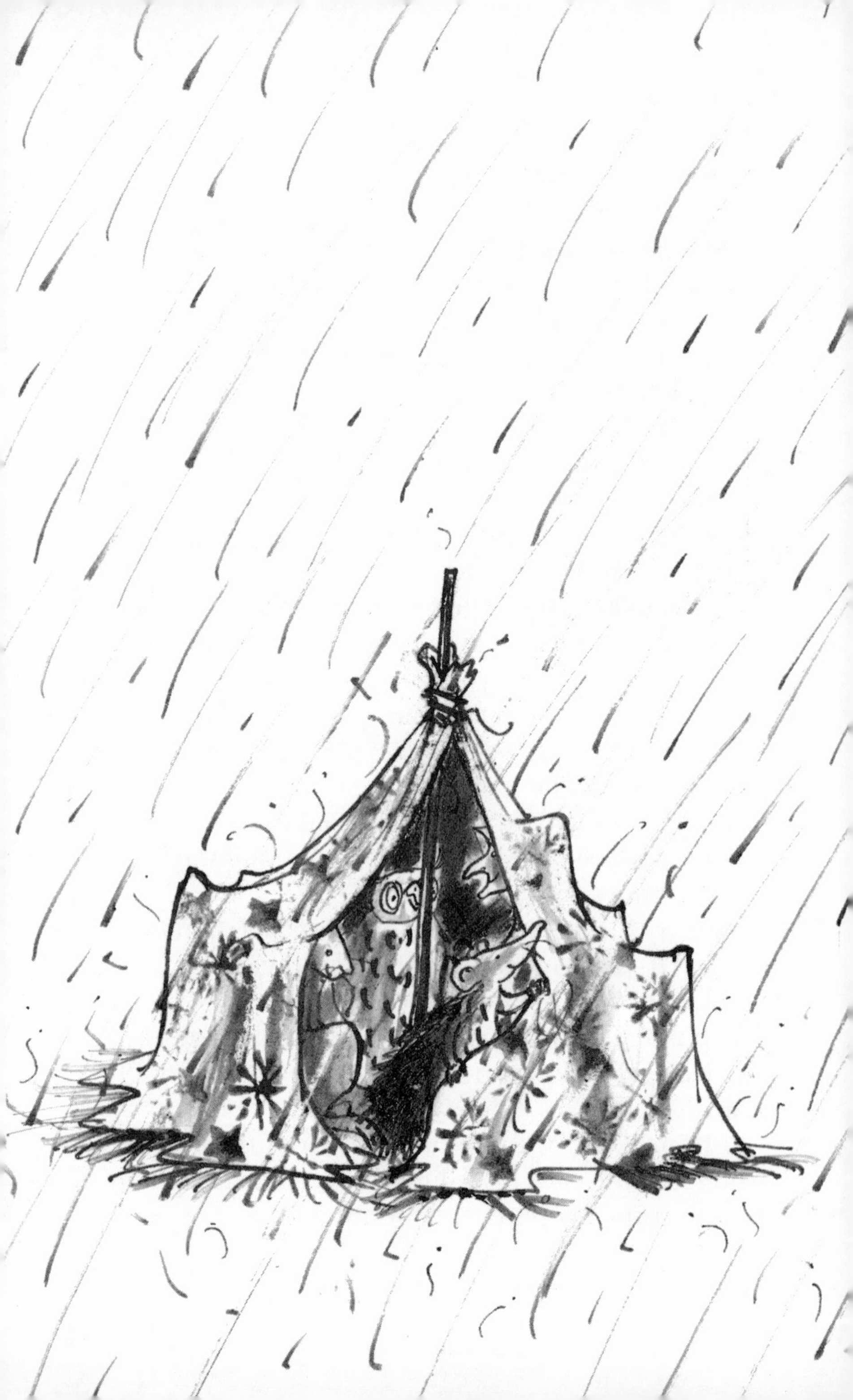

"There's more pie," said the witch.

"I felt a drop," said the hare.

"Me, too," said the owl. They looked up. "It's raining!"

"The apple pie's getting wet!" cried the hedgehog. "We have to put up the tent! Hand over that broom!"

He grabbed the broom and stuck it into the ground again.

The hare and the owl pulled the curtain up over it and a moment later they were all sitting in the tent.

"You see what a good tent it is?" said the hedgehog.

The witch didn't answer. She looked at the owl, who was chewing, deep in thought.

Suddenly the owl leaped up. "I remember my poem!" He leaned toward the witch. "Your special poem, madam."

The witch beamed. She smiled at the hedgehog and said, "It's a very good tent."

The hedgehog smiled back. "And a very good apple pie." He quickly took the last piece. "Let's hear it, Owl!"

A GOOD DEED

The hare was sitting in the shadow of the beech tree, reading a book.

"Hi, Hare!" said the hedgehog.

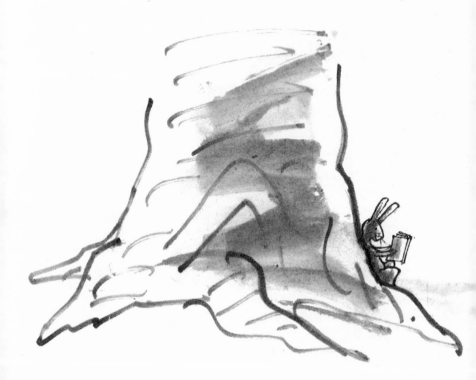

"Hi," said the hare without looking up.

"Are you reading?"

"Mmm."

"Is it exciting?"

"Mmm."

"What's it about?"

The hare sighed and looked up. "About a hare who sets off into the wide world."

"Is there a hedgehog in it?"

"No."

"Too bad. It would be even more exciting if there were a hare and a hedgehog in it. What does the hare do in the wide world?"

"Good deeds," said the hare. "He rescues a sick beaver, he repairs a pheasant's house, he helps old animals, and lots more."

The hedgehog tugged at the hare's arm. "Shall we go out and do good deeds, too?"

"Fine with me," said the hare. "But I'm reading now." And he went on reading.

"Then I'll start by myself," said the hedgehog. He disappeared into the forest at a trot. Watchfully he looked around to see if anybody needed help.

In the clearing he saw the crow with a branch in his beak.

"Are you fixing your house?" asked the hedgehog.

The crow nodded.

"Just hand me that branch," said the hedgehog. "I'll help you."

The crow dropped the branch. "You?"

"Sure. I'll fix your house in a jiffy."

The crow began to laugh. "How are you planning to do that? My house is over there." He pointed at the top of a huge tree.

"Oh," said the hedgehog disappointedly. "I can't reach that."

The crow picked up the branch again and flew to the tree.

The hedgehog walked on. Above his head he heard someone cough. He looked up hopefully.

The squirrel was sitting on a branch eating nuts.

"Are you sick?" the hedgehog inquired.

"Sick?" asked the squirrel. "Well, no!"

"But I heard you coughing!"

"I choked on a piece of nut."

The hedgehog smiled reassuringly. "Don't worry. I'll save you."

The squirrel looked down in surprise. "Save me? Why?"

"Because you're sick."

"I'm not sick!" shouted the squirrel and he started throwing nuts at the hedgehog.

"Then I won't come save you," said the hedgehog, insulted, and he walked on.

He reached the wicked witch's cabin. He wanted to keep going, but all of a sudden he stood still.

"The witch is getting old," he said pensively.

He paced back and forth in front of the door. Then he knocked. He heard nothing.

Carefully he pushed the door open.

The witch wasn't in, but over the fire a cauldron simmered. On the table lay mushrooms and greens and turnips.

The hedgehog walked over to the cauldron and, filled with curiosity, peeped over the rim.

"Magic potion," he said with distaste. He picked up a ladle. "I'll finish it for her. That's a good deed all right."

He took the mushrooms, greens, and turnips from the table and tossed them into the cauldron. He stirred it all up. The potion started boiling and bubbling, and a thick cloud rose up out of the cauldron. The hedgehog pinched his nose shut. He gave it another good stir.

"Ready!" he said contentedly. "How happy she'll be!" He put the ladle away and skipped outside. I'll just run over and tell the hare."

The hare was still sitting there reading.

"I did a good deed!" the hedgehog shouted from a distance. "I helped the wicked witch!"

The hare snapped his book shut, alarmed. "The wicked witch? Did she think it was all right?"

"She doesn't know yet," chuckled the hedgehog. "She wasn't home. But I finished making her magic potion for her."

"So you know how?"

"Course I do. It isn't hard at all. Just throw everything in and stir well."

"Sure, sure," said the hare. "I see."

"Soon she'll be home," the hedgehog said, aglow, "and everything will be ready. How thankful she'll be."

"I hope so . . . ," the hare said with a sigh.

The hedgehog looked at him in surprise. "What do you mean?"

"Ooyooyooy!" trumpeted through the forest.

"That's what I mean," said the hare. He jumped up and shoved the hedgehog behind the beech tree. "Sit there and stay!"

"Why?" asked the hedgehog.

But the wicked witch was already steaming up. "Have you been in my house?"

"No," said the hare and he showed her his book. "I've been reading all afternoon."

"Who was in my house then?"

The hedgehog leaped out all radiant from behind the beech tree. "Me!"

The witch came at him, seething. "You again! I should have known! Ooyooyooy!"

The hedgehog took a step backward. "I—I finished making your magic potion for you," he stammered. "Aren't you happy?"

"Happy?" screeched the witch. "That magic potion was finished! And now it's unusable. Totally spoiled! Botched!"

"But those mushrooms and turnips were supposed to go in, weren't they?"

The witch stamped her feet. "They were my supper!"

"Oh . . . ," said the hedgehog, dismayed.

"My supper gone and my magic potion spoiled! I'll make you pay for that!"

"I just wanted to help," whimpered the hedgehog. "Just ask the hare."

"He really did want to help," said the hare. "It was a good deed."

"A good deed," sniffed the witch. "Then I know of a good deed, too. I'll turn him into a stag beetle, then I won't be pestered by him again."

"Help!" squeaked the hedgehog. "Don't!"

"He meant well," the hare quickly added. "And you can easily make another magic potion, can't you, ma'am?"

"Not this one," sighed the witch. "That's the whole point. There were rare herbs in it and they're all used up now. It'll take years for me to collect them all again."

"Boy," said the hare sympathetically. "No wonder you're angry."

The witch sniffed. "And my supper's gone, too.

What am I supposed to eat for supper now?"

The hare patted her hand. "Ma'am, you can come and have a nice supper at my place. The hedgehog and I will make something tasty for you."

"Something better than those turnips," said the hedgehog.

The witch's face brightened. "Yes . . . That would actually be very nice."

"Agreed," said the hare. "We'll come get you when it's ready."

"Until this evening, then," said the witch. She started to leave, but the hedgehog tugged on her skirt.

"That magic potion I finished—what was it for, anyway?"

"That magic potion you botched, you mean?" snarled the witch. "It was for turning animals into gravel." She shuffled off.

For a moment it was quiet. Then the hare walked over to the hedgehog and shook his hand.

"Thank you," he said. "It was a good deed after all."

SAILING ON THE POND

The hedgehog and the blackbird were walking along the pond and looking at the water.

"If only we had a boat," said the blackbird.

"Yes . . . !" said the hedgehog. "Let's build one!"

"Much too difficult," said the blackbird. He thought for a moment. "But a raft would of course be possible . . ."

Slowly they continued along the edge of the water.

Suddenly the hedgehog stood still. "There! There's our boat!"

Half out of the water stuck a wide board. They ran over to it.

"We can easily fit on it together," said the blackbird. "Now, a pole."

"What for?"

"To push the boat."

"I know where there's a stick," the hedgehog cried. He disappeared among the trees and returned with a long, sturdy branch. "Is this one good?"

"Perfect," said the blackbird. "Let me have it."

Together they pushed the board into the water. They stepped onto it and there they were, bobbing on the pond.

"It works!" shouted the blackbird. "We're sailing!"

"Yoho yohee," sang the hedgehog. "We're sailing on the wild sea."

"You call this a wild sea?" The blackbird smirked. "Not the tiniest wave in sight."

The hedgehog rocked back and forth. "If we rock, it's a wild sea."

"Stop it," said the blackbird in distress. "I'm getting seasick."

He stuck the branch into the water and pushed. The board slowly glided forward.

"Faster!" shouted the hedgehog. "Can't you sail faster?"

"No," panted the blackbird. "This is heavy work."

When the board was in the middle of the pond, the blackbird sat down. "Phew! Now it's your turn."

The hedgehog took over the branch. "Watch out. Now we're going to go fast!"

He pushed so hard that the board shot forward. The hedgehog lost his balance and fell, branch and all, into the water.

"Help!" he hollered, thrashing around. "Hedgehog overboard! Help, help!"

"Swim!" yelled the blackbird. He fished the branch out of the water. "Here. Grab it."

The hedgehog grabbed the branch. The blackbird pulled him over and helped him climb up.

"Brrr, that water sure is cold," said the hedgehog, shivering.

"Why did you act so crazy, then?" the blackbird growled.

"I wasn't acting crazy," said the hedgehog plaintively. "The boat tipped and I just fell—*kerplunk!*—in the water."

He shook the water off his spines and took hold of the branch again. Carefully he pushed the board forward.

"That's the way," said the blackbird. "Now you've got the hang of it." He sat down at the stern of the board and looked at the water.

"Yoho yohee," the hedgehog sang softly. "We're sailing on the wild sea. Yoho yohee . . ."

The blackbird closed his eyes. Suddenly he felt a jolt. Startled, he looked around. "What have you done this time?"

"The boat's stuck," said the hedgehog. "Give me a hand."

The board was wedged among the waterplants.

"Why don't you watch where you're going," groaned the blackbird.

"I was supposed to sail! I can do only one thing at a time."

The blackbird took over the branch and tried to wrench the board free. "It's stuck fast. This won't work."

"Maybe if we push at the same time," said the hedgehog. "I'll count to three. One, two, three!"

Crack! The branch broke in two.

In dismay they looked at the short stick they were holding.

"And now this," sighed the blackbird. "Now we'll never get out of here."

The hedgehog sat down. "What should we do?" he asked in a small voice.

The blackbird shrugged. "I can just fly away. But you . . ."

"You aren't leaving, are you?" the hedgehog asked anxiously.

"I'm going to get help. And then I'll be back."

"Then go quickly."

The blackbird stretched his wings and flew away.

The hedgehog watched him go until he couldn't be seen anymore. Then he looked at the water and the shore in the distance.

"All alone," he said softly. "In the middle of the wild

sea." He threw up his hands, covered his eyes, and waited.

The blackbird flew as swiftly as he could to the hare's. Together they went to the pond.

"There he is," said the blackbird, pointing at the hedgehog huddled on the board.

"Hedgehog!" the hare shouted across the water. The blackbird whistled shrilly.

The hedgehog looked up and waved. "You finally got back?" he called.

"We're coming to rescue you!" shouted the hare.

"But how?" asked the blackbird.

The hare rubbed his chin. "Hmm . . ."

"Hurry it up a little!" the hedgehog hollered. "I'm getting cold."

"Now, if we had a long rope," said the blackbird, "then I could attach it to the board and we could easily pull him over to the side."

"We don't have a long rope," said the hare. He looked around. "Hey . . . !"

"Do you see a long rope?"

"No. But I do see somebody who might be able to help."

In the distance was the wicked witch, walking with a bundle of sticks under her arm.

The hare and the blackbird cupped their mouths and yelled as hard as they could, "Witch! Wi-hitch!"

The witch came shambling up with her sticks. "What's the matter?"

"The hedgehog's stuck in the plants," said the hare, pointing. "There, in the middle of the pond."

"On a board," the blackbird filled in. "We went sailing."

The witch burst out laughing. "Heehahoo! That figures—for the hedgehog. Heehahoo!"

The hare pulled at her sleeve. "Madam, could you conjure him over to the shore?"

"Is anything happening over there?" the hedgehog called out. "It'll be dark soon."

The witch looked at the sky. "First I'm going to

collect some more wood, as long as there's light. Then I'll conjure him back."

She was going to walk away. The hare held her back. "But he can catch cold."

"Or drown . . . ," said the blackbird.

The witch grew pale. She laid her sticks on the ground and mumbled a spell. Instantly the board shot free of the plants.

"Hurrah!" cheered the hare and the blackbird.

But then they fell silent, in fear. The board was racing across the water, heading straight for the shore.

"Watch out!" shouted the blackbird.

At the last minute, the board veered and again raced across the water.

"What are you doing now, ma'am?" asked the hare.

"I'm letting him sail a bit more," chuckled the witch. "To cure him of it. Otherwise I'll have to rescue him again tomorrow."

The board skimmed around the pond in a cloud of spray and spatters.

"Hold on tight!" the hare called out.

The blackbird was nervously hopping up and down.

Finally the board started to slow down. It made one more trip across the pond, then approached the shore and lay there.

The hare and the blackbird ran over to the hedgehog.

"How are you doing?" the hare inquired worriedly.

The hedgehog stood up. Beaming, he looked at the witch. "That was nice and fast! May I go again?"

"No," the witch said shortly. "And give me that board, I can use it for firewood."

"No way!" cried the hedgehog. "That's my boat! Tomorrow I'm going sailing again."

"Tomorrow we'll collect firewood for you," the hare promised the witch. "And thank you for rescuing the hedgehog."

Muttering, the witch picked up her bundle of sticks from the ground and shuffled into the forest.

The hare and the blackbird helped the hedgehog onto dry ground.

"Did you see how fast I can go?" the hedgehog demanded proudly.

"You didn't do that," said the blackbird, "the wicked witch did."

"She helped out a little," admitted the hedgehog. "But tomorrow I'll do it all by myself. Yoho yohee . . ." He skipped off home.

The hare and the blackbird watched him go.

"We should probably collect wood by the pond tomorrow," said the hare.

"With a long rope," said the blackbird.

THE SPUTTER LAMP

One evening the hare had just made some tea when there was a loud banging on the door. With the teapot in hand, he opened the door.

The owl and the hedgehog were standing on the doorstep.

"Ah, Hare. We're just in time, by the looks of it."

"Yes," said the hare and he held up the teapot. "I just made some tea." He looked outside. "What a dark evening. No moon, no stars . . . Were you two able to find your way all right?"

"I was," said the hedgehog. "I can see everything in the dark."

"Me too," said the owl. "I don't need the moon or the stars."

"Now I can see a star," said the hare and he pointed with the teapot. "There."

The owl and the hedgehog turned around.

"That certainly is a big one," said the owl.

"It's moving!" said the hedgehog.

"That's impossible," said the hare.

"It *is* possible. Just look."

"It's coming this way," the owl said nervously.

"How strange," said the hare. "Is it really a star?"

"It's the moon," said the owl shrilly. "The moon fell down."

"There isn't any moon," said the hare. "This is something else. It looks like a lamp." He took another good look. "It *is* a lamp."

The lamp slowly came closer.

"It's looking for us," whispered the hedgehog. "I'm going home."

The hare held him back. "We'd better stick together. Maybe it's dangerous."

The lamp was now very close. The animals were standing in a bright light and they could hear a sputtering sound.

"The world is coming to an end," said the owl hoarsely.

The hedgehog covered his eyes with his hands and peered between his fingers.

The hare took a step forward.

"Stay here!" cried the owl. "It could be dangerous."

The hare wasn't listening. He was squinting up. "Come and look. The lamp is hanging on a rope!"

"On a rope," the owl said, barely breathing. "It's come to this."

"But if it's hanging on a rope," said the hare pensively, "then it's attached to something."

"Attached to something," the owl said, nodding. "Just what I was going to say. But to what?"

"To the wicked witch," said the hedgehog. "Want to bet?"

"That could well be . . . ," said the hare.

Above the crackling they could hear chuckling. The lamp shot up, flew in a little circle above the hare's house, and slowly came down again.

"You see?!" shouted the hedgehog. "It *is* the witch. With a lamp on her broom."

A rope had been fastened to the witch's broom, and on that rope hung a lantern that gave bright light and made loud popping sounds.

The witch landed next to the house. "I saw you all standing there!" she cackled. "I could see you from far, far away."

The hare pointed with the teapot at the lantern.

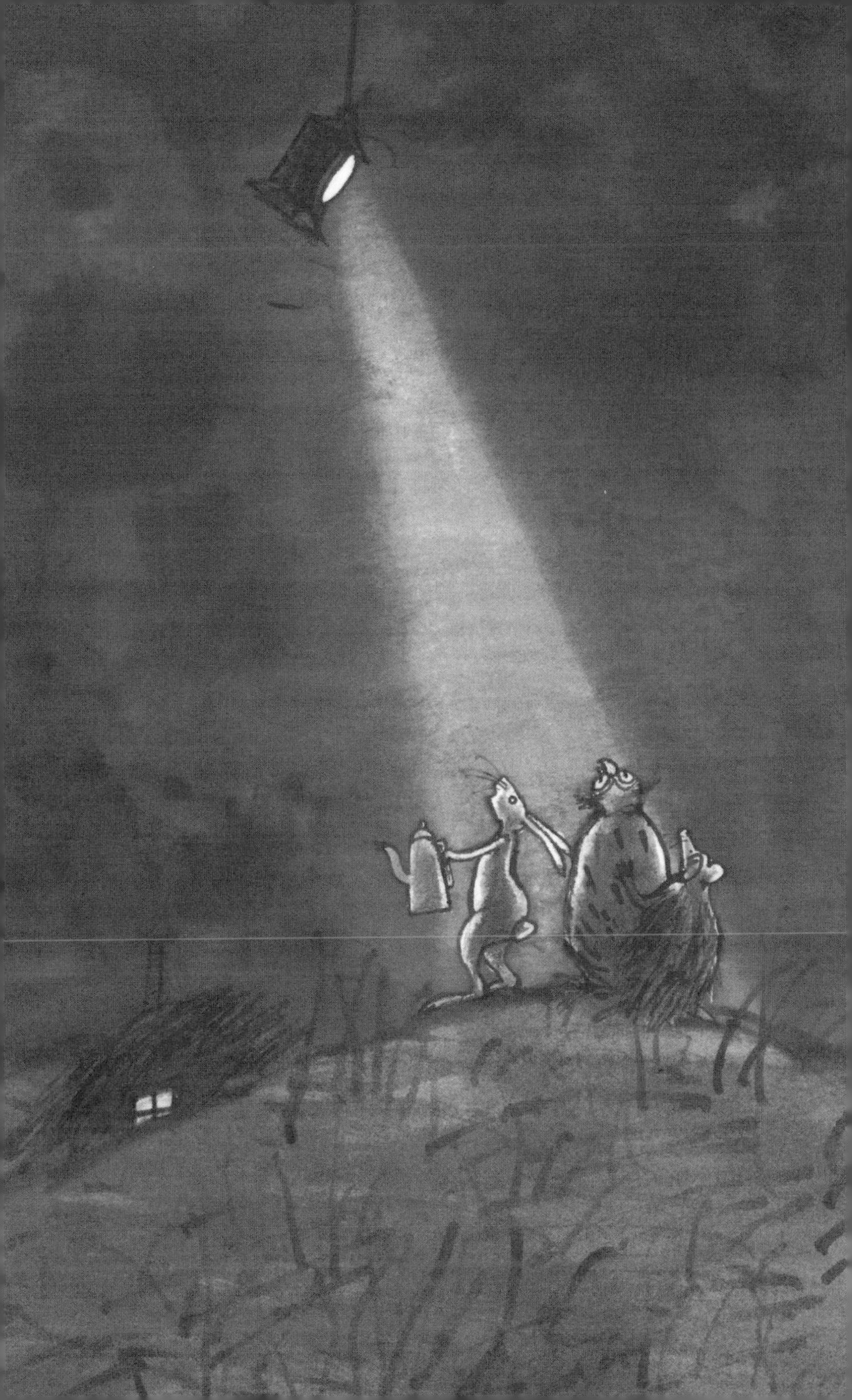

"What's that?" he asked.

"A witch's lantern, a real sputter lamp. So at least I can see something when I'm flying in the dark."

"You don't need a lantern for that, do you?" asked the owl. "I can see everything in the dark."

"Me too," said the hedgehog.

"But *I* can't," said the witch. "Now I can finally see everybody. Nobody will be able to escape me anymore, heeheehee."

The hare and the owl looked at each other nervously.

"That light's shining right in my eyes," complained the hedgehog. "Could you turn it off?"

"No," said the witch. "A sputter lamp burns all the time. At least if it doesn't rain." She looked up at the sky.

"It can't take water?" the hare asked.

"No. It'll go out if it gets wet and then I'll have to conjure up a new one."

"It's not going to rain," said the hare. "Honestly, it's not." He held the teapot up. "We were just about to drink some tea. Would you like a cup, too, ma'am?"

The witch hesitated.

The hare nudged her into the house. "Owl, give the witch a chair. Hedgehog, will you put on some water? I'll be right in."

He tiptoed over to the sputter lamp and emptied the teapot. Sputtering and sizzling, the light went out. The hare quickly jumped inside the house and closed the door.

"I'm going to make some fresh tea!" he said in a festive voice.

"Well," said the witch after her third cup, "it's time I got going."

The owl stood up. "I'm going to go home, too."

"Me too," said the hedgehog.

The hare went outside with them. The witch shuffled over to her broom but suddenly stood still. "It's dark!" she said.

"Of course," said the hedgehog. "That's the way it always is at night."

"My sputter lamp is gone!" exclaimed the witch. "It's been stolen. Ooyooyooy!"

"It's lying over there," the owl pointed. "On your broom, madam. But it's gone out."

The witch ran over to the lantern and bent down. "It's wet! That's why it's out." She looked up.

"Then it did rain," said the hare. "I wouldn't have expected that."

"But the ground is all dry," said the hedgehog.

The hare poked him. "A local shower," he said and winked at the owl.

"Very local," said the owl. "A single cloud."

The witch looked quizzically at the hare. "How strange that it should have rained right on my lamp."

"Very odd," the hare said gravely.

The owl nodded.

"Out of my way, all of you," growled the witch and she picked her sputter lamp up off the ground. "I'm going to conjure up a new one right away."

The hare cleared his throat. "Do you really think you should do that?"

"Yes, of course. Then at least I can see you all well."

"But," said the hare, "if you can easily see us with that lamp, madam, then we can see you easily, too."

"Yes!" cried the hedgehog. "We saw you coming miles away."

The witch turned pale. "Did you all see me coming?"

"Of course," said the owl. "A light that moves like that stands out. You can see it anywhere."

"I hadn't thought of that," mumbled the witch.

"But *we* did," said the hedgehog. "We think of everything."

"From now on, all the animals will know exactly where you are at night, ma'am," said the hare.

"Absolutely not!" screamed the witch. "That won't happen! I won't conjure up a new sputter lamp after all." She mumbled something and the lantern vanished immediately.

"Very wise," said the hare, smiling.

"It was a bother to fly with," the witch said with a sigh. "The rope kept catching in the branches." She went and sat down on her broom. "But now I have to fly in the dark again. Bah."

"I'll fly in front of you, madam," said the owl. "I'll bring you home."

He waved to the hare and the hedgehog and flew away. The witch flew after him.

"Well, well," said the hare with satisfaction. "We're rid of that miserable lamp anyway."

"What a stroke of luck that it rained," said the hedgehog. He looked down at the ground. "But the ground's dry all over. How can that be?"

"I'll show you," said the hare. He ran inside and came back with the teapot.

"A local shower," he said and he turned the teapot over.

The hedgehog looked wide-eyed at the teapot. Then he grinned a big grin. "We sure are smart," he said.

DREAM POTION

The hedgehog sat on the edge of his bed and stretched.

"What a strange dream," he said. "I have to tell the others about it."

He went outside and walked into the forest. In the clearing he spotted the owl.

"Owl!" he called out.

The owl didn't hear him. He continued slowly, mumbling to himself.

"Owl! I had a strange dream last night! I dreamed—"

"*High above the trees . . . ,*" mumbled the owl.

"I dreamed that I was helping the witch with a magic potion and—"

"Dreams!" said the owl. He stood still and said solemnly:

> "*High above the trees*
> *flew I in my dreams.*

"That's it. Thank you."

"I dreamed of this magic potion," the hedgehog said

pointedly, "and I still remember exactly—"

"A very nice dream," said the owl. "Tell me the rest when my poem's done." And he started mumbling again.

The hedgehog heaved a sigh and kept walking. "I'll go see the hare. At least he doesn't make up poems."

The hare was sitting in front of his house talking with the blackbird.

"You have to listen to this!" cried the hedgehog. "I had such a strange dream!"

The hare and the blackbird kept talking.

The hedgehog stood right in front of them. "Hey! I dreamed that—"

"We're talking," said the blackbird. "About serious matters."

"My dream is serious, too."

"Dreams are deceptions," said the blackbird.

"What did you dream about?" inquired the hare.

"About the witch."

The blackbird laughed scornfully. "Is that what you came here to bother us about?"

"The witch and I were making a magic potion together. And I can still remember exactly what went into it. Chestnut shells and—"

The hare shifted back and forth impatiently. "We're busy right now. Why don't you tell us another time."

"Go tell the witch," said the blackbird, joking. "Maybe she'll be able to use it."

The hedgehog stamped his foot. "All right," he said angrily. "I *will* go to the witch."

He turned around and walked to the wicked

witch's cabin.

The cabin door was open. The witch was sitting at the table reading her book of magic spells.

"Witch!" the hedgehog called out. "I dreamed about you."

"Good," said the witch and kept reading.

"We were making a magic potion together."

"What nonsense."

"And I can still remember exactly what went into it."

The witch looked up from her book. "Oh, really? What was it?"

"Chestnut shells and twisty grass . . ."

The witch snapped her book of magic spells shut. "Chestnut shells and twisty grass," she said pensively. "That could be. And what else?"

"Devil's thistle and chives," said the hedgehog. "And licorice."

"Licorice?"

"Licorice. That was very important."

The witch looked at him wide-eyed. "What was this magic potion for?"

"I don't know," said the hedgehog. "Before it was done, I woke up."

The witch got up. "I'm going to try it right away."

"Try what?"

"That magic potion, of course! And you can help."

The hedgehog flushed with pride. "And they were saying that dreams are deceptions!"

◆ ◆ ◆

The hare and the blackbird were still talking when the owl flew up. "Do you two smell anything?" he asked.

The hare and the blackbird sniffed the air.

"It smells a little odd," said the hare.

"It stinks," said the blackbird. "What is it?"

The owl pointed at a cloud of smoke in the distance. "The witch is making a magic potion. And I have the impression the hedgehog is helping her."

"The hedgehog?" the hare and the blackbird said in unison.

"Yes. I was walking along thinking about a poem and then I ran into the witch and the hedgehog carrying a basket full of herbs. And a little later I saw that smoke coming out of her chimney."

The hare looked at the blackbird. "Would the hedgehog really tell the witch his dream?"

"Don't think so," said the blackbird. But his voice sounded uncertain.

"Dream?" asked the owl. "He said something to me, too, about dreams this morning."

"He dreamed about a magic potion," said the hare.

"And he's making it now," said the blackbird.

The hare stood up. "Come on. We'll go have a look."

They walked quickly to the witch's cabin. The door was shut and dark smoke billowed out of the chimney.

"What a stench," said the blackbird, making a face.

The hare pushed the door open. The witch and the hedgehog were both stirring something in the big cauldron.

"What are you here for?" demanded the witch.

"We're busy," said the hedgehog. "Tell us some other time."

The hare pointed at the cauldron. "Is that the magic potion from your dream?"

"Yes," said the hedgehog proudly. "I could still remember exactly what was supposed to be put into it. It's almost ready."

"And then?" asked the owl. "What's that dream potion for?"

"We don't know yet, but we'll find out," snickered the witch. "You can all have a taste, heeheehee."

The hare and the owl and the blackbird shrank back and ran outside.

"Taste!" gasped the owl. "I'd have to be crazy!"

The hare looked at the witch's cabin. "The hedgehog is in danger," he said.

"How so?" asked the blackbird.

"If we're not around, the witch will obviously have him taste it. And who knows what will happen then . . ."

"It's his own fault," said the blackbird. "He shouldn't have told the witch his dream."

"It was your idea," said the hare.

The blackbird turned pale. "That's—that's not how I meant it," he stuttered.

"We have to rescue him before it's too late," exclaimed the owl nervously.

"We'll go get him," said the hare. "Follow me."

He walked back to the cabin. The others followed hesitantly. "Hedgehog!" shouted the hare. "Come quick! That potion could be dangerous."

"No, it isn't," said the hedgehog. "I dreamed it myself."

"And mind your own business," snapped the witch.

"But maybe you'll turn into something awful or get sick," insisted the hare.

The hedgehog wasn't listening. He stirred the pot wildly.

The dream potion began to boil and get foamy.

"Watch out!" cried the witch. "It's boiling over!" She grabbed the hedgehog and yanked him back.

The potion bubbled up, churned over the rim, and ran sizzling into the fire. When the steam had cleared, there was nothing left but a muddy layer on the bottom of the cauldron.

"I thought so," said the witch peevishly and she threw her ladle to the floor. "Not a real magic potion. If you dream something again . . . !"

"How do you know, ma'am, that it wasn't real?" asked the hare.

"A real magic potion doesn't boil over."

"But in my dream it was real," said the hedgehog. He scooped a spoonful of sludge from the pot.

"Don't do that!" cried the owl.

"Don't taste it!" shouted the hare.

The hedgehog blew on the spoon and stuck it into his mouth.

Speechless with fright, the others watched.

"Brr, yuck!" shuddered the hedgehog. He waited. "Nothing's happening!"

The animals breathed a sigh of relief.

"That's what I said, didn't I?" said the witch. "Not real!"

The hedgehog looked glumly at the cauldron. "Maybe there should have been more licorice in it . . ."

"Shut up," growled the witch. "I shouldn't ever have listened to you. Dream potion. Bah!"

"I told you so right away," said the blackbird. "Dreams are deceptions."

"Usually they are," said the hare. "But not always."

The others looked at him questioningly.

"Now I remember what I dreamed last night," said the hare. "I dreamed about pancakes."

"Pancakes!" said the owl. "I suddenly feel hungry."

"I dreamed that you all came over to eat pancakes. What do you say?"

"Let's do it," said the blackbird.

"At least that's a dream that's practical," said the witch.

"Did you dream about a lot of pancakes?" asked the hedgehog.

"Piles!" said the hare.

"First one at the hare's house!" shouted the hedgehog and he ran outside.

HIDE-AND-SEEK

The hare and the hedgehog sat under a tree.

"Shall we do something?" asked the hedgehog.

"All right," said the hare. "Shall we run?"

"Run!" said the hedgehog with a look of disgust. "I do that only when the wicked witch is after me."

"Throw chestnuts, then?"

"We did that yesterday."

"Hide-and-seek?"

"Yes!" cried the hedgehog and he jumped to his feet. "You're It!"

The hare stood with his face to the tree and started counting. "Ten, twenty, thirty, forty . . ."

The hedgehog ran off. While running he looked for a place to hide, but no spot seemed good enough. He passed the wicked witch's cabin.

". . . eighty, ninety, one hundred—here I come!" came the voice from the distance.

"He's coming already," panted the hedgehog. He ran to the side of the cabin and crawled behind the rain barrel.

"Are you looking for something?" asked the witch.

"I'm looking for the hedgehog," replied the hare. "We're playing hide-and-seek."

The witch's hand shot to her mouth. "Are you two really playing hide-and-seek?"

"I told you so!" shouted the hedgehog.

The hare looked up. "Hedgehog! How did you get up on the roof?"

"The witch got me up here by magic," moaned the hedgehog. "And I'm dizzy. I'm going to fall off."

The hare looked at the witch reproachfully. "What did you do that for, ma'am?"

The witch lowered her eyes. "He was behind my rain barrel. I thought he wanted to steal something from my cabin."

"Me?" exclaimed the hedgehog indignantly. "And all the time I kept saying we were playing hide-and-seek."

"I thought that was a story."

"We really are playing hide-and-seek," said the hare. "Do some magic and get him down quickly."

"Hurry up!" said the hedgehog. "I'm dizzy."

The witch mumbled a spell.

Nothing happened.

"How can that be?" said the witch, amazed. "I'll try again." She pinched her eyes shut and mumbled the spell.

"Is anything happening down there?" The hedgehog stamped his foot. "I'll fall off in a minute."

"Isn't it working?" asked the hare.

A moment later he heard footsteps. He made himself as small as possible and held his breath.

"Hola!" a shrill voice shouted. "What are you doing behind my rain barrel?"

The hedgehog looked up. The wicked witch stood looking at him suspiciously.

"What are you doing here? Are you planning to snitch something from me?"

"Shhh!" whispered the hedgehog. "Otherwise the hare will know where I am."

"So what?" asked the witch. "Why shouldn't he know where you are?"

"You don't get anything, do you!" said the hedgehog with a sniff. "We're playing hide-and-seek. That's the honest truth."

The witch began to chuckle. "Is that right? But then I know a much better spot for you. He'll never find you there."

"Where's that?" asked the hedgehog.

"I'll show you," chuckled the witch. "Pay attention."

She mumbled something and suddenly the hedgehog was sitting on top of the cabin.

"Help!" cried the hedgehog. He looked down fearfully. "Get me off! I'm getting dizzy!"

"You're going to sit there for a while," said the witch. "That'll teach you to snitch things from me." She walked toward the door.

Just then the hare came running up.

"Ah, Witch!" he called out and looked behind the rain barrel.

"No," said the witch. "Could I have remembered that spell wrong? I'll just take a peek in my book of spells." She shuffled inside.

"Now I might have to stay here forever," said the hedgehog in a small voice. "And I'm so dizzy already."

"Don't worry," said the hare. "If she can't remember the spell, then we'll just get a ladder."

The hedgehog's face brightened. "Of course she can always come get me with her broom!"

"If you're dizzy you shouldn't go sit on a broom. Much too dangerous."

"It's already getting better," the hedgehog said quickly. "And you can really hold on to a broom."

The witch shuffled outside. "I remember it now! One of the words was wrong just then."

"Don't bother," said the hedgehog.

The witch mumbled something, and there was the hedgehog, on the ground again.

"Thank goodness!" said the hare.

"Too bad," grumbled the hedgehog. "I'd rather have come down on the broom."

"Are you still dizzy?" asked the hare.

"Just a little bit."

"Then I'll bring you home," said the hare. "We'll play hide-and-seek another time."

"It's suddenly all gone," said the hedgehog. "We can play hide-and-seek right now."

The hare looked at the witch. "Would you like to play, too, ma'am?"

"Me?" exclaimed the witch. "Hide-and-seek? At

my age?"

"Why not? You can walk fast and you're good at finding people."

"You found me right away," said the hedgehog.

"That's true . . . ," said the witch.

The hedgehog gave her a nudge. "You're It!"

"But—" the witch started to object.

The hare and the hedgehog were already gone.

The witch hesitated for a moment. Then she stood with her face to the door and began to count. "Ten, twenty, thirty, forty . . ."

HOPPING DROPS

The hedgehog and the blackbird were on their way to the hare's. When they passed the wicked witch's cabin, the blackbird peered in through the half-open door.

"The witch has made some currant juice," he said.

"Currant juice?" blurted the hedgehog.

"Yes. Yesterday she was out all day picking. And look, now there are all these full bottles on the table."

The hedgehog looked. "She always makes really delicious currant juice," he said pensively.

"Hm," said the blackbird.

The hedgehog stood where he was. "Shall we go say hello?"

"Say hello? Why?"

"No reason. It would be nice."

"I'd watch out," said the blackbird. "Before you know it, she's back doing some magic and that isn't so nice."

"I'm going to go in for a minute anyway," said the hedgehog. "You go on ahead to the hare's. I'll be right there."

"That's your own business," said the blackbird. "See you soon. I hope." And he continued on his way.

The hedgehog pushed the door open farther. "Ah, Witch. How's it going?"

The witch was sitting at her table with a glass of currant juice. "What do you want?" she inquired.

The hedgehog walked up to her. "I'm so thirsty."

"Get yourself a glass of water."

The hedgehog looked at the bottles. "Something else would be all right, too . . ."

"I'm beginning to get the picture," said the witch, chuckling. "Do you want some currant juice?" She took a glass and filled it. "But go look outside first to see that nobody's coming. If the others see you getting juice, then they'll all want some and it'll be gone much too quickly."

The hedgehog walked outside.

The witch quickly snatched a small brown bottle off the table and put a few drops in the glass.

The hedgehog returned. "I didn't see anybody."

"That's good. Here, just drink this down."

The hedgehog emptied the glass and licked his lips. "May I have another glass?"

"Of course you may."

The hedgehog drank another glass of juice and sighed with contentment.

"Not thirsty anymore?" asked the witch.

"No," said the hedgehog. "Thank you. I have to go to the hare's now. Bye!"

He was going to walk to the door, but walking didn't work. He could go only in little leaps.

"Hey!" cried the hedgehog, scared. "I can't walk normally. I'm sick!"

The witch burst out laughing. "Heehahoo! You're not sick. You can hop very well."

The hedgehog balled up his fists. "Did you put something in that juice?"

The witch held up the little bottle. "Hopping drops! It makes you hop like a sparrow. Boy, that's a good laugh."

"A real hoot," said the hedgehog. "But now you've had your laugh. Let me walk normally again."

"No," said the witch. She got up. "You go on now. I have more to do here." She pushed the hedgehog outside and closed the door.

"I'll make you pay for this!" shouted the hedgehog. "Just you wait!" He turned around, then hopped off through the forest toward the hare's house.

The hare and the blackbird were sitting in front of the door. In surprise they looked at the hedgehog, hopping along the path.

"What are you up to now?" asked the hare.

"You look like a kangaroo," said the blackbird.

"The witch!" puffed the hedgehog. "The hop! The drops!"

"Sit down right now," the hare said with concern. "What happened? How come you're jumping around so strangely?"

The hedgehog sat down. "Hopping drops," he said, out of breath. "Phew! That sure makes you tired."

The hare and the blackbird looked at him questioningly.

"The witch put hopping drops in my currant juice," the hedgehog explained. "From a little brown bottle. And now all I can do is jump."

"Has she completely lost her marbles?!" the hare said indignantly.

"I did warn you," said the blackbird. "But you had to go say hello to the witch."

"I think it's mean," sniffed the hedgehog.

"I do, too," said the hare. "Come on, Blackbird, we're going to have a talk with the witch."

"You really think we should do that?" asked the blackbird. "She's in a bad mood today."

"No, she isn't," said the hedgehog. "In fact, she

really had to laugh."

"Laugh!" said the hare bitterly. "At somebody else's hopping around. We're going to see her right now."

With long strides he walked to the wicked witch's cabin. The blackbird had to fly to keep up with him.

Without knocking, the hare entered the cabin.

The witch was sitting at her table sticking labels on the bottles.

"Witch! You had the hedgehog drink hopping drops."

The witch looked up. "So what?"

"You don't do things like that," the hare stated sternly.

"You do if you're a witch," chuckled the witch. "And now, outside with you two, I'm busy."

The hare stood beside the table. "We'll go as soon as you make those drops stop working."

"That's impossible," said the witch and she took a sip of currant juice.

The hare and the blackbird eyed each other worriedly.

"But it isn't necessary," continued the witch. "It'll pass by itself."

"When?" asked the blackbird.

"I don't know. It varies a lot. The effects disappear after an hour with some and with others it can last a couple of days."

"A couple of days!" exclaimed the hare. "Poor Hedgehog."

The witch looked at him in surprise. "What difference does it make anyway? What's so bad about having to hop?"

"You should try it yourself sometime," grumbled the blackbird. "Then you'd talk differently."

The hare gave the blackbird a nudge and pointed at a small brown bottle that stood next to the big bottles. The witch filled her glass again. Then she got up to put the bottle of juice in the cupboard.

The hare quickly took the little brown bottle from the table. But the witch was approaching the table again.

The hare held the bottle behind his back. The blackbird began to whistle under his breath.

"Hey," said the hare. "What's that I see outside? It looks like a parrot!" He gave the blackbird a poke.

"Yes," said the blackbird. "Now I see it, too. A parrot."

"That's impossible," said the witch. "There are no parrots around here."

"But I really do see one," said the hare. "A red parrot. Go see for yourself."

The witch walked over to the window and looked out.

The hare shook a couple of drops into the witch's glass and put the little bottle back.

"I don't see any parrot," said the witch.

"Then maybe it was a squirrel," said the hare.

"Or a red-breasted robin," said the blackbird, grinning.

"You two are pulling my leg!" screeched the witch. "Off, back home with you two. And quickly!"

The hare and the blackbird went outside.

"When will she notice?" asked the blackbird.

The hare swallowed. "Let's walk a little faster."

When they were close to the hare's house they heard someone shouting, "Hare! Blackbird! Look!" The hedgehog was running toward them. "It's over! I can walk normally again!"

"Thank goodness!" said the hare. "It could have lasted a couple of days."

"I'm curious how long it will last for the witch," said the blackbird with a chuckle.

"For the witch?" asked the hedgehog.

"The hare put hopping drops in her glass."

The hedgehog laughed with satisfaction. "Perfect!"

"We have to hide," said the hare. He looked over his shoulder. "She'll be here soon."

He had barely finished his sentence when the animals heard a whizzing sound above the trees. The wicked witch flew up on her broom and landed right in front of the hare.

"You put hopping drops in my glass!" she shouted so loudly that her voice cracked. "That's why I was supposed to look at that parrot. Ooyooyooy!"

The hare bounded away.

The witch chased him with little jumps.

"Ha, ha!" shouted the hedgehog and the blackbird. "A skipping witch!"

"Stay there!" gasped the witch. "Or I'll turn you into an aphid!"

The hare stopped. "But why are you so angry, ma'am?" he asked. "It isn't bad at all having to hop around. You said so yourself."

"Now at least you know what you put the he[dge]hog through," said the blackbird.

The witch didn't know what to say for a min[ute]. Then she looked at the hedgehog from the corner of [her] eye and mumbled, "It *is* bad. All that jumping ma[de] you dead tired."

"Yeah," the hedgehog complained. "Absolut[ely] dead tired. I'm done in."

The witch bowed her head.

The hare patted her on the shoulder. "The hedge[]hog's over it already, so it probably won't last long f[or] you either. And until it's over, you've always got yo[ur] broom. That way it shouldn't bother you."

The witch nodded and sighed. She hopped back t[o] her broom.

The hedgehog tugged at her skirt. "May I sit on th[e] back? I'm *so* tired from all that jumping."

The witch hesitated. "No," she said finally.

"Oh!" cried the hedgehog. "Oh, this is terrible! It['s] come back!" and he hopped back and forth.

The witch looked around. "That's impossible."

"Is not," moaned the hedgehog. "Just look." H[e] winked at the hare and the blackbird.

"A relapse," said the hare. "That's always possible[.]"

The blackbird nodded. "I've often heard it said."

"I'm getting exhausted again," puffed the hedge[]hog. "Could you bring me home on your broom?"

The witch looked at him suspiciously. Then sh[e] looked at the hare and the blackbird. They looked bac[k,] their faces serious.

"Oh, go ahead," the witch said at last. "Have a seat."

"Ahoy, ahoy, ahoy!" cheered the hedgehog and he danced around.

"Aha!" shouted the witch. "Didn't I know it? You *are* over it!"

The hedgehog quickly sat down behind her on the broom. "It cleared up a little just then," he said in a weak voice. "Bring me home, quick, then I can rest."

The witch mumbled something and the broom went up into the air. The hedgehog waved proudly at the hare and the blackbird.

"Sit still!" the witch said peevishly.

The hedgehog held on to the witch as they flew over the trees to the hedgehog's house.

"He succeeded," said the blackbird in admiration, "in getting the witch to agree."

"The witch had to make up for something," said the hare. "And she won't be making any more hopping drops for a while, I'll bet. You?"

THE STILL-LIFE

The hare opened the door wide and carried a small table outside.

On the table he put a bowl with apples in it. Then he took his sketchbook and his pencils and sat in front of his door.

He looked long and thoughtfully at the bowl and began to draw.

"Green," said the hare quietly. "And red. And a little brown, here . . ." He started humming to himself.

"Hare!"

Reluctantly the hare looked up. The hedgehog came running up.

"The wicked witch is chasing me," he panted.

"Why?"

The hedgehog looked down at the ground. "She was gathering herbs and I threw sand in her basket and then she got mad."

"Is it any wonder?" asked the hare.

"I'm going to stay here for a bit," the hedgehog said quickly. "And if the witch comes, you can stop her."

The hare sighed. "All right. But you'll have to keep

your mouth shut because I'm drawing."

"I won't say a thing," promised the hedgehog. He pointed at the sketchbook. "That needs more red."

"I know," said the hare, irritated. "I haven't gotten that far." He kept drawing.

"May I have an apple?" asked the hedgehog.

"No!" said the hare. "Then my still-life won't be the same anymore."

"Your *what*?"

"My still-life. That over there."

"I thought that was a fruit bowl," said the hedge-hog, taken aback.

"It is. But if you're making a drawing of it, it's called a still-life. You can have an apple when it's done."

"Draw quickly, then," said the hedgehog.

"I can do that only if you keep your mouth shut," growled the hare.

The owl came flying up. "Hi there! What are you drawing?"

"A still-life," said the hedgehog. "Or don't you know what that is?"

The owl looked over the hare's shoulder. "Very nice! But wouldn't it have been better if you'd placed the bowl in the middle?"

"No," the hare said curtly.

"I'm allowed to say something, aren't I?" inquired the owl.

"You're not allowed to say anything," said the hedgehog. "Otherwise he can't draw."

The owl nodded. "I can understand that. When I'm

thinking of a poem, others aren't allowed to disturb me, either."

The hare turned around. "Could you two go talk somewhere else? I can't work like this."

"We're already going," said the hedgehog, insulted. "Come on, Owl."

They walked away.

The hare heaved a sigh of relief.

But there they were again. "The wicked witch is coming!" shouted the hedgehog.

"That's all I need," grumbled the hare.

The witch came stomping up. "I finally got you, Hedgehog. Throwing sand in my basket! Ooyooyooy!"

The hedgehog hid himself behind the hare. "Stop her!"

"Quiet!" shouted the hare. "Let me draw in peace for once!"

The witch stood where she was and looked at the sketchbook. "Did you draw that? How clever. Those apples seem real."

"Thank you, madam," said the hare, smiling.

The witch pointed at the table in the drawing. "You only need to add something on the side. It's so bare now."

"I'm not going to add anything," said the hare, gritting his teeth. "Nothing whatsoever."

"You aren't supposed to talk to him," said the hedgehog.

"He can't work if you do," explained the owl.

"You can see he's working on a still-life, can't you?"

said the hedgehog. "But of course you don't know what that is."

"I do so!" snapped the witch. "And I've still got a little bone to pick with you. Sand in my basket! I'll turn you into an apple worm!" she threatened as she went for the hedgehog.

"Don't!" squeaked the hedgehog. He leaped backward and knocked into the table. The table teetered, and the bowl slid to the edge and fell on the ground with a crash. The apples rolled every which way.

"Watch what you're doing," snapped the owl. "That beautiful bowl, in pieces!"

The hedgehog pointed at the witch. "It's because of her! *She*—"

The hare threw his sketchbook on the ground and jumped up.

"That does it!" he thundered. "First you all keep me from my work with your quibbling, and now you go and smash my fruit bowl to smithereens. Go away, all of you!"

With bowed heads, the hedgehog and the owl moved away.

"Wait a minute," said the witch. She picked up one of the pieces from the ground and tossed it on the table. In an instant the bowl was standing on the table again, with all the apples in it. And beside the bowl there was an apple pie.

The hedgehog and the owl ran back. Wide-eyed, the hare stared at the table. "My fruit bowl is whole again!"

"Not a crack to be seen," said the owl. "And what a beautiful pie."

"The witch can divide it up," cried the hedgehog.

"In a little while," said the hare and he picked up his sketchbook. "First I'm going to draw it in."

"I told you something needed to be added on the side," said the witch with a chuckle.

"Can I have an apple, then?" asked the hedgehog.

"Shhh!" hissed the owl and the witch.

Everybody was quiet and the hare drew the pie beside the fruit bowl.

"There we are," said the hare a while later. "My still-life's done." He held up the sketchbook.

"Bravo! Great! So lifelike!" the others cheered.

The hare stroked his whiskers with satisfaction. "And now, apple pie," he said. He went to get a knife and the witch cut the pie into wedges.

The hedgehog took a big bite. "Mmm," he said. "This is the most delicious still-life I ever tasted!"

BOO

The owl sat under a tree, dozing. Something rustled behind the tree, but he didn't hear it.

"Boo!" somebody yelled right by his ear.

The owl awoke with a start and struggled to his feet.

The hedgehog came out from behind the tree, laughing. "Were you scared?"

"I was scared to death," said the owl shakily. "I was almost asleep."

"There's the hare," said the hedgehog. "Don't say anything!" He disappeared behind the tree again.

"Come on, don't do that," the owl called out. "It isn't funny."

The hare came over carrying a bucket. "What isn't funny?"

"Boo!" said the hedgehog from his hiding place.

"Ah, Hedgehog," said the hare.

The hedgehog peered out disappointedly from behind the tree trunk. "How did you know it was me?"

"Well . . ." The hare waved his bucket. "I'm going to pick blackberries. Do you two want to come?"

"I'm going to stay here for a while," said the hedge-hog. "I'll come later."

"We'll save some blackberries for you," said the hare as he walked off with the owl.

The owl looked back. "He's behind the tree again. I'm sure he's planning on scaring more animals."

The hare nodded. "As long as he doesn't do it to the wicked witch."

"He wouldn't do that, would he?" said the owl. "*That* . . ."

"Boo!" they heard in the distance. And right after-ward, a shrill voice, "Ooyooyooy! Miserable prickly creature! I'll hex you plum purple with gold around the edges!"

"Here we go," sighed the hare.

"They're coming this way," said the owl.

The hedgehog came barreling up. "Out of my way! Let me through!" He ran by and disappeared to the left of the path among the trees.

And then came the witch. "Where did the hedge-hog go?"

"Over there," said the hare, pointing to the right.

"Well, she's out of the way for a while," said the hare. "So at least the hedgehog can hide somewhere."

"Then he'd better hurry up," said the owl. "Because there she is again."

The witch came back and grabbed the hare and the owl by their shoulders. "Where is the hedgehog?"

"Over there," said the hare. "That's what I said, isn't it?"

"He isn't there," snapped the witch, stamping her foot. "You sent me the wrong way on purpose."

"Did you look carefully?" asked the owl.

"Yes. And he's not there."

"Funny," said the hare, "I saw him going that way myself."

"Me, too," said the owl. "I was just saying, 'There goes the hedgehog.'"

"Lies!" growled the witch. "I don't believe a word of it."

"The hedgehog has surely found a good place to hide. You'll never find him anyway. Why don't you come join us? We're going to pick blackberries." He pulled the witch along.

"That rude creature," said the witch, peeved. "Saying boo to the wicked witch! How dare he! If I get him in my clutches, I'll . . ." She stopped in her tracks. "What's that I hear?"

From somewhere in the forest came the sound of singing:

> *"As long as a hedgehog has his spines*
> *there is nothing for him to fear."*

"I hear a bird," declared the hare loudly.

"A cooing dove," said the owl.

"Or it could be a nightingale . . ."

"Or a cuckoo . . ."

"You can stop now," said the witch. "I recognized his voice all along. Singing! He dares to sing, after what he did!"

"A soul without any cares," said the hare dreamily.

"Not for long," said the witch grimly. "I'll hex him plum purple."

She was about to run off. The hare stopped her. "Wait! I have a plan."

"A plan to let the hedgehog escape again, you mean."

"No," said the hare. "A plan to make him pay for saying boo." He whispered something into the witch's and the owl's ears.

The witch chuckled. "Good. And then I'll hex him plum purple."

"There he comes," said the owl.

"Behind that bush," whispered the hare. "I'll count to three."

The hedgehog sauntered up with a spring in his step.

"As long as a hedgehog has—"

"BOO!"

"M-mercy!" hiccuped the hedgehog and he rolled backward in panic.

The others came out from behind the bush.

"Heehahoo!" the witch sang out. "The hedgehog is scared of 'Boo'!"

"I bit my tongue," whimpered the hedgehog. "I almost can't talk anymore."

"It'll be nice and quiet," chuckled the witch. "You

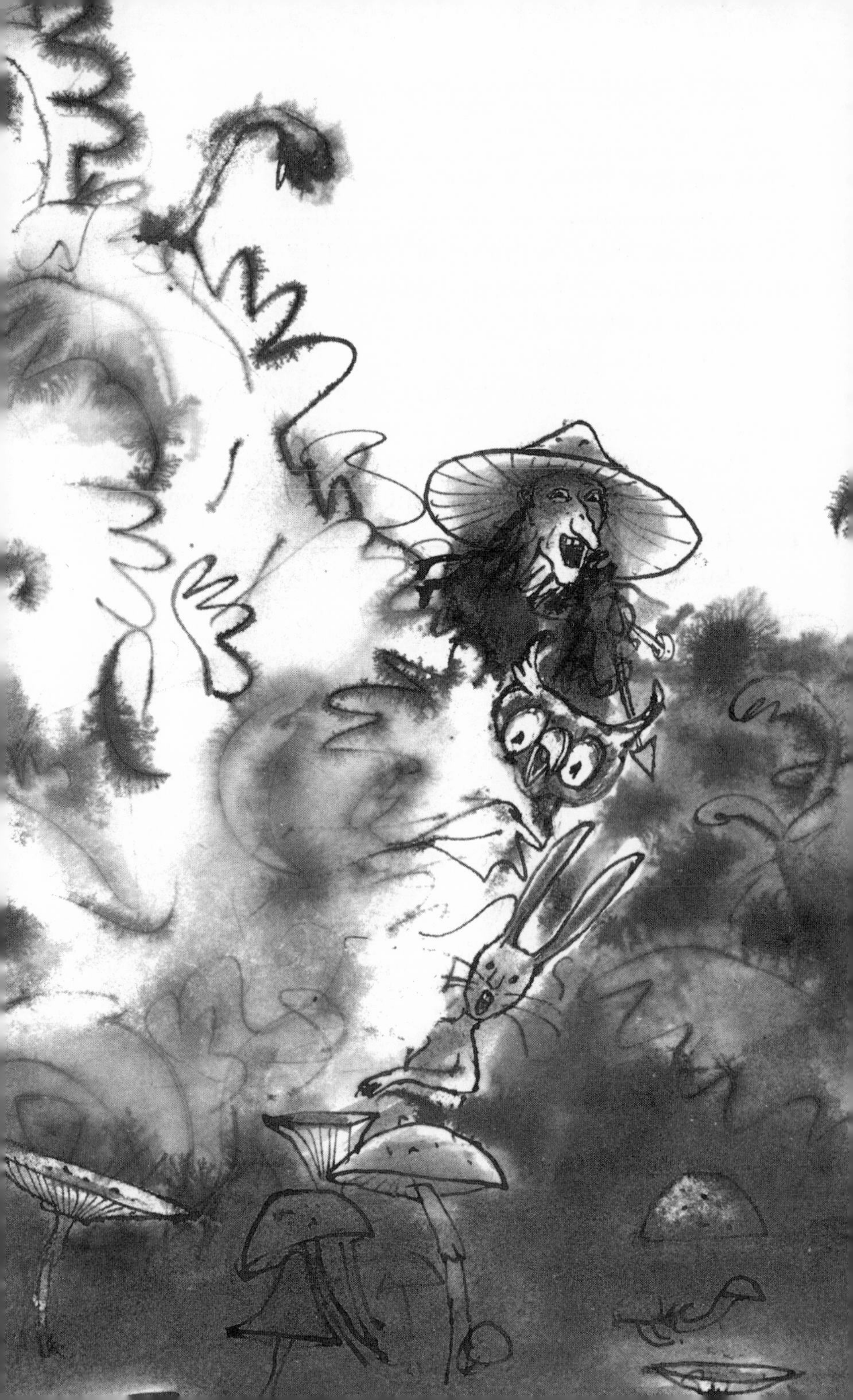

won't be able to shout 'Boo.' And now I'm going to turn you plum pur—"

"Not on your life!" said the hare. "He scared us and we scared him, we're even. And besides, ma'am, you're not angry anymore."

"Oh, really?" cried the witch.

"No. You were laughing, and if someone is laughing, that person isn't angry anymore."

The witch thought for a moment. "That's true . . ."

The hare waved his bucket. "And now we're going to pick blackberries!"

"And eat blackberries!" said the owl.

"Then we'll turn plum purple all by ourselves," giggled the hedgehog.

THE HEDGEHOG GOES ADVENTURING

One morning, very early, the hare was running through the forest.

"Everybody's still asleep," he said with satisfaction. "I'm the only one who's outside already."

He heard something. He stood still to be able to listen better. Somebody was singing.

"As long as a hedgehog has his spines
there is nothing for him to fear."

"The hedgehog!" the hare said in surprise. "So early?" He ran in the direction of the singing. "Hedgehog! You're out and about early. That's not like you."

"Today it is," said the hedgehog. He looked around and whispered mysteriously, "I'm going on a long, dangerous journey."

"Where to?"

"I don't know. That's what's dangerous. I'm going on an adventure."

"Shall I come along?"

"No. I want to go on an adventure all by myself."

"When are you coming back?"

"This afternoon."

"Oh," the hare said, relieved. "I thought you'd be gone for a lot longer than that."

"Of course not," said the hedgehog. "I have to eat, don't I?"

"See you this afternoon, then," said the hare. "And be careful."

"I'm always careful," said the hedgehog and he went on his way, singing.

The hare was about to start running again when he heard a whooshing noise. He turned around and there was the witch, sheering right by his head on her broom.

"Watch out!" the hare shouted in alarm.

The witch waved, grinning, and flew higher.

"And here I am thinking nobody's awake," moaned the hare. "I think I'll go home. It's far too busy here."

As evening fell, the hare went over to the hedgehog's house. "I have to hear all he's been through."

He knocked. There was no response.

The hare pushed the door open. "Hedgehog?"

It was very quiet inside.

"He'll be here soon," said the hare. He sat down by the door and waited.

When he had been waiting for a quarter of an hour, he couldn't bear it anymore. He jumped up and ran to the owl's tree.

The owl was sitting on a branch talking with the blackbird.

"Have either of you seen the hedgehog?" the hare called up.

"The hedgehog?" said the owl. "No, we haven't all day."

"He's off on an adventure," said the hare. "He left early this morning, and he still hasn't come back."

"Where did he go?" asked the blackbird.

"I don't know. But he should have been back long ago. I'm afraid something's happened."

"Maybe he got lost," said the blackbird.

"Maybe he fell," said the owl. "Or maybe he was taken prisoner, or . . ."

"All right, all right," said the hare nervously. "We have to go look for him."

"But where?" asked the blackbird. "If we don't even know where he went . . ."

The hare thought for a moment. "Maybe the witch will know. She was flying around early this morning. Come on!"

A short while later they walked into the wicked witch's cabin.

The witch was sitting in her chair, napping.

"Witch!" shouted the hare. "Ma'am, do you know where the hedgehog went?"

The witch started from her sleep. "What's happened to the hedgehog?"

"He's gone. He left very early . . ."

"On an adventure," said the owl.

"And he still hasn't come back," said the blackbird.

The witch yawned. "I did see him out walking this morning, but where he went I don't know."

"We're so worried," said the hare.

"The hedgehog isn't a babe in the woods," said the witch.

"But he should have been back a long time ago," said the hare.

"Most likely, he has lost his way," said the blackbird.

"Or hurt himself," said the owl. "Or had a bad accident."

"We have to go look for him," said the hare. "Will you help us look, ma'am?"

"Help you look?" cried the witch. "Do you know how early I was up this morning?"

"Just as early as I was," said the hare.

"And just as early as the hedgehog was," said the blackbird.

"Who is now lying in the forest hungry and hurt," said the owl.

"All right, all right, all right," sighed the witch, "I'm coming already." She got up stiffly and reached for her broom.

"Good!" said the hare and he nudged her outside. "Madam, you will fly over the entire forest on your broom. Owl, you go that way. Blackbird, you look over there. I'll run along all the paths. As soon as it gets dark, we'll all come back here."

"*With* the hedgehog, we hope," said the owl in a low voice.

The hare ran through the forest. He looked in ditches and in bushes, but the hedgehog was nowhere to be found.

The hare ran around the forest one more time. He asked all the animals he met, "Have you seen the hedgehog?" But no one had seen him.

It grew dark.

The hare looked in at the hedgehog's house once more, but it was dark and silent.

"I give up," sighed the hare. Tired, he went back to the witch's cabin.

The owl was already there. He looked at the hare inquiringly, then shook his head.

The witch came flying up and landed in front of the door. "And?" the hare and the owl burst out at once.

"I didn't see him anywhere," said the witch and she leaned her broom up against the wall.

"But where can he be?" the owl mumbled anxiously.

The witch sat down beside him. "As long as nothing bad happened," she said dejectedly.

"If the blackbird hasn't found him, either," said the hare, "then we'll start looking right away again." He drummed on the ground. "Where is that blackbird, anyway? It's completely dark already."

"Quiet," said the owl. "I hear something. That'll be the blackbird."

"Hi there!" someone shouted right behind them. "What are you all doing?"

"We're waiting for—" the hare started to explain. He spun around. "Hedgehog!"

The owl and the witch jumped to their feet.

"Hedgehog! Where were you? What happened? We were so worried!"

The hedgehog looked in surprise from one to the next. Then he looked serious.

"I have to sit down for a minute," he said softly. "I've been through a lot."

The others stepped aside respectfully.

The hedgehog sat down. "I thought I'd never see any of you again."

"But what happened?" exclaimed the hare. "What all did you go through?"

The hedgehog began, "All kinds of things! Lost my way, was hungry and thirsty, and then bush thieves . . ."

"Bush thieves?" said the owl with a shudder. "Here? In our forest?"

The hedgehog nodded.

"What did these bush thieves look like?" asked the hare.

"I don't know. They were behind a bush."

"What did they do?" asked the witch.

"They demanded, 'Who's there?' in a really mean voice."

"Terrible," sympathized the owl.

"And when I ran away as fast as I could, they called, 'Hedgehog! We're looking for you!' Again in that mean voice. They know who I am!"

"Terrible," said the owl, beside himself. "Then you're in danger. They'll come after you for sure."

"And then?" asked the hare.

"Then I crept into a hollow tree until I didn't hear anything anymore."

"How smart," said the witch. "You are a smart little hedgehog."

The hedgehog nodded proudly.

The hare rubbed his chin, thinking hard. "Hm. Still, I wonder . . ."

"Don't you believe there were bush thieves?" asked the hedgehog indignantly. "I heard them myself, didn't I?!"

"Hey!" The blackbird came flying up. "Here you are!" he called, out of breath. "Where did you get to so quickly?"

"What do you mean?" asked the hedgehog.

"I was looking for you and I heard something behind a bush. I called, 'Who's there?' and then I saw

you bolt away."

The hare and the owl looked at each other. The witch began to chuckle.

The hedgehog turned red and looked down at the ground.

"I even called out, 'We're looking for you!' But I couldn't see you anywhere anymore."

The hare smiled. "He was in a hollow tree."

"Why?"

"Because of the bush thieves," explained the owl.

"Bush thieves?" the blackbird asked in surprise. "What bush thieves?"

The hare patted him on the shoulder. "Never mind. The hedgehog's back again, and I think he'll be hungry after his adventure."

The hedgehog looked up. "My stomach's growling!"

"Mine, too," said the blackbird.

"Yes, now that you mention it . . . ," said the owl.

The witch walked to the door. "I've got a big pot of soup." She held the door wide open and chuckled. "Come in, but hurry, because I'm as hungry as a bush thief!"

THE WICKED WITCH GOES SKATING

The hedgehog sat sleeping in his chair in front of the heater. He woke up when a knock came at the door.

"C'min," he called out sleepily.

The hare and the owl came in. "Are you coming with us to the pond?"

"Close the door," said the hedgehog. "What are you going to do at the pond?"

"Go out on the ice," said the hare. "The pond is all frozen and the ice is thick enough. I already tried it early this morning."

"I'm staying here," said the hedgehog.

"Why?"

"It's so cold!"

"No, it isn't," said the owl. "If you walk fast it isn't."

"Oh, come on," said the hare. "The pond doesn't freeze all that often."

The hedgehog got up with a yawn and put on his scarf. "All right, then."

They walked outside.

"Brrr," shivered the hedgehog.

"The sun's out," said the hare. "It's beautiful weather."

"It's cold," said the hedgehog.

"Keep walking," said the owl. "That'll warm you up automatically."

They walked quickly to the pond.

"Look at that," said the owl. "Somebody's here already."

The wicked witch was sitting on the edge, tying up her skates.

"I'm going back home," said the hedgehog.

"You aren't scared of the witch, are you?" asked the hare.

"No, but my spines are cold."

The hare kept walking. "Hello there, ma'am!" he cried. "What fine skating weather we have today."

The witch looked around. "What are you all doing here?"

"We're going to go out on the ice," said the hare. "Just like you."

"As long as all of you stay out of my way, because I want to do some skating."

The witch stood up and wobbled onto the ice. She glided forward a short distance, then flailed her arms and fell down on the ice with a thud.

The hare and the owl rushed over and helped her up.

"How can that be?" muttered the witch. "I used to be able to do it so well."

"You just have to get used to it again," said the hare.

The witch nodded and out of the corner of her eye looked at the hedgehog, who was standing hunched

over on the shore. "You're not standing there laughing at me, are you?"

"I *can't* even laugh," the hedgehog complained. "My cheeks are frozen."

"Skate," said the hare. "We'll hold on to you."

The witch stretched her legs stiffly.

"It's already getting better," said the owl.

The witch carefully skated along the edge of the pond.

"Now I've got the hang of it again," she said, red from the exertion.

The hare and the owl let go of her and off she went, left, right, left, right, straight across the pond.

"Good going!" shouted the hare and the owl.

The hedgehog stepped falteringly onto the ice. "Cold!" he said.

"Just look at the witch!" cried the owl. "See that?"

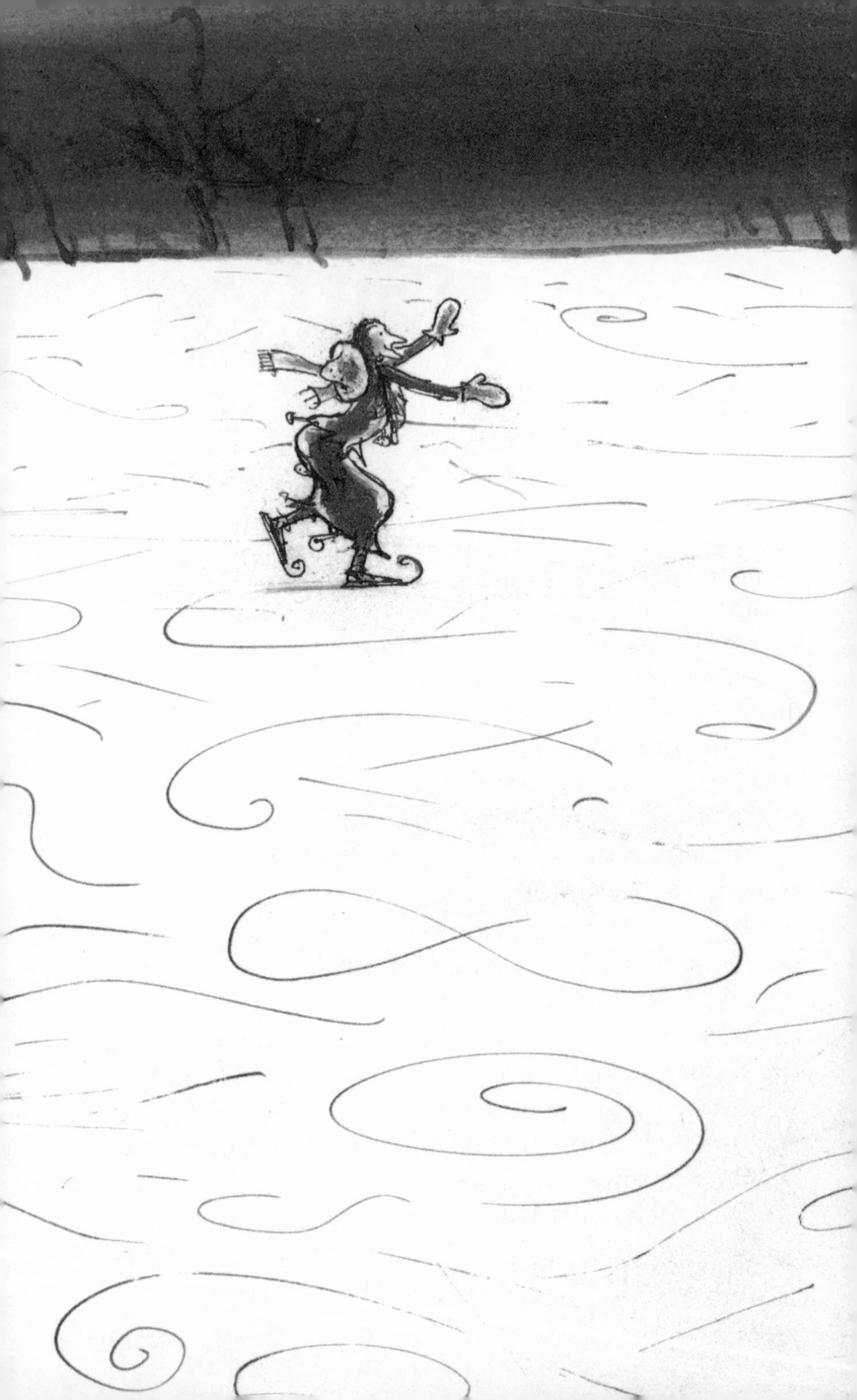

The witch was turning circles on one leg.

"Yes," said the hedgehog and he hunched farther down into his scarf.

The witch skated back with long strokes and started doing figure eights.

The hare and the owl clapped. The hedgehog blew on his hands.

"Clap!" said the owl. "Your hands will warm up that way."

The witch skated off.

"Let's make a sliding place!" exclaimed the hare. He took a running start and slid across the ice. "The ice is nice and smooth!"

The owl followed him.

The hare slid back again. "You come, too!" he shouted at the hedgehog.

The hedgehog lifted one foot, then the other. "No . . ."

"It'll warm you up," said the owl breathlessly.

"I won't ever be warm again," said the hedgehog. "Ever."

The hare and the owl walked over to him and took hold of him. "Here you go. Do it just once."

The hedgehog looked undecidedly at the sliding lane.

The hare and the owl gave him a push and there he went, sliding on the ice.

"Ohhh!" he exclaimed. "Whoa! I can't stop!"

"You'll stop automatically!" the hare shouted back.

"Yes!" the hedgehog said in amazement. He turned

around. "See how far I went? Much farther than either of you!"

He slid back.

"Now us again," said the owl.

"We'll play who gets the farthest," said the hedge-hog. "I'll be the last one."

The owl took a running start and slid down the lane.

The hare followed him and stopped a good distance farther.

"Now me!" shouted the hedgehog. "Look out!" He took a very long running start.

Just then the wicked witch skated closer. She put her arms out to the side and reached one leg back.

"Watch out!" yelled the hare.

"Out of my way!" squeaked the hedgehog. "I can't stop!"

The owl closed his eyes.

The hedgehog slammed full speed into the witch. He lost his balance, the witch fell over him, and together they slid toward the hare and the owl.

The hare pulled the witch up on her feet. "Did you hurt yourself, ma'am?"

The witch stamped her skate and immediately lost her balance again. The hare and the owl caught her just in time.

"Idiot!" screeched the witch. "Can't you watch where you're going?"

"I couldn't stop!" whimpered the hedgehog. "Honest, I couldn't."

"And I was skating so well . . ."

"Yes," said the hare quickly. "How well you skate!"

"Superbly!" said the owl. "I couldn't believe my eyes."

The witch flushed and lowered her eyes. "I still have to practice a little," she said. Then she gave the hedgehog a dark look. "Clumsy spiny creature! Who goes ice sliding when somebody's skating?"

"It was to get warm," the hare explained. "The hedgehog was cold, so we had to keep him moving."

"He tends to get cold," said the owl.

The hedgehog regarded him indignantly. "I don't tend to get cold at all. In fact, I feel hot!"

The hare coughed. "We were all cold," he said.

The witch took her skates off. "I'm getting cold, too, now that I'm standing still . . ."

"Then you should slide on the ice, too!" exclaimed the hedgehog and he gave her a hard shove down the lane.

"Eekeekeek!" shrieked the witch.

"What are you doing?" said the hare in alarm to the hedgehog.

"You two did that to me when I was cold, didn't you?" said the hedgehog.

"Yes, but . . . ," stammered the owl.

The witch slid to the end of the lane. She turned around and headed for the hedgehog, swinging her skates. "And now I'm going to turn you into an icicle! How dare you push me!"

"That was to get warm," squeaked the hedgehog. "Sliding on the ice warms you up."

The hare quickly pulled him over to the edge. "Running fast warms you up a lot more," he said. "Now, run!"

THE WICKED WITCH
HAS A BLAST

The hedgehog walked sleepily through the forest. Suddenly he stood still. He heard something.

"An explosion!" said the hedgehog. "What's going on now? They aren't shooting, are they?"

Pow! There was the same sound again. This time it sounded closer.

The hedgehog hid in some ferns. A moment later he heard shuffling footsteps.

"I thought so," grumbled the hedgehog. "The wicked witch is out having a blast."

Carefully he peered through the ferns. The witch shambled by and tossed something green on the ground. *Pow!* A white puff of smoke spiraled up.

When the witch was gone, the hedgehog crawled out of the ferns and looked around on the ground. But he couldn't find anything.

Pow! That was right behind him.

"Mercy!" squeaked the hedgehog and turned around.

"Don't be so curious, little hedgehog," chortled the

witch. "I saw you."

"Will you quit it?" gasped the hedgehog. "What are you throwing, by the way?"

"Poweepeas," said the witch.

"Poweepeas? And what are they?"

"They're normal peas I've cast an itty-bitty spell on," the witch said with a chuckle. She took a handful of peas out of her apron pocket.

"Look. At home I've got a whole bucketful."

"May I try, too?" asked the hedgehog.

"Well, all right," said the witch. "Because you had such a fright just then."

The hedgehog snatched all the peas from her hand.

"Just *one*!" cried the witch. "Not all of them!"

But the hedgehog had already disappeared in the ferns.

"Greedy prickly creature," said the witch peevishly. "If I catch you, I'll turn you into a gall wasp."

Pow! A pea exploded right in front of her feet.

"Ooyooyooy! How dare you!"

"You started!" shouted the hedgehog and he was gone.

The witch walked on, complaining to herself.

The hedgehog skipped the other way and threw poweepeas on the ground. He still had two left when he saw the hare and the owl approaching. The hedgehog hid behind a tree. When the hare and the owl were quite close, he threw a pea on the path.

Pow!

"Help!" hiccuped the owl and he flapped backward.

"What's going on?" the hare asked, looking pale.

The hedgehog appeared, spluttering. "Poweepeas," he said.

"Where did you get them?" asked the hare.

"I got them from the witch. Look, this is my last one." *Pow!*

"Is that all?" asked the hare. "A bang and a bit of smoke?"

"It's fun," said the hedgehog. "It makes you laugh."

"I don't laugh at something like that," said the owl. "I'm going home."

"Wait a minute," said the hare. "I hear something." *Pow! Pow, pow!*

"The witch is blasting them," said the hedgehog. "*She* thinks it's fun."

The hare covered his ears. "This has to stop," he said. "There are sick animals and old animals and animals who want to sleep . . ."

"It'll be a while yet," said the hedgehog.

"The witch has a bucketful of those things at home. At least, that's what she said."

"A bucketful? We'll have to do something about that." The hare thought for a moment. "If she's here blasting peas, then we can go over to her cabin to have a look. Come, quick."

They hurried to the wicked witch's cabin. The hare looked around, then carefully pushed the door open. "Aha!" he said. "There they are."

On the floor stood a bucket filled with green peas.

"They look very normal," said the owl.

The hedgehog picked a pea out of the bucket and threw it on the floor.

Pow!

"Don't do that!" said the owl in alarm. "She could hear us."

The hedgehog looked anxiously at the door. "I only wanted to know if they worked . . ."

"Help me carry this," said the hare. "We'll take the bucket."

"What do you want to do with it?" asked the owl.

"I don't know yet. As long as they're not here."

"Could have a blast," the hedgehog said quietly. The owl gave him a stern look. "I'll hold the door open," the hedgehog said quickly.

The hare and the owl carried the bucket to the door. The hedgehog held the door wide open.

Pow! A poweepea exploded on the doorstep.

"And another one!" yelled the wicked witch. *Pow!* "I heard you all!"

"Stop it," said the hare, "or we'll tip the bucket over."

"Don't do that!" cried the witch. "My house will blow up."

She mumbled a spell. "There. They won't explode anymore. And now tell me what you are all doing in my house. What are you hauling that bucket around for?"

"We wanted to take those exploding things away," explained the hare. "You can't use them in a forest."

"I can't? And why not?"

"Because there are sick animals and old animals and animals who want to sleep."

"Oh," said the witch in dismay. "I hadn't thought of that." She sighed. "All right, I won't fire anything off anymore."

The hedgehog took a pea from the bucket and threw it outside. "Let's just make sure they really don't work."

The pea rolled away.

"It didn't go off!"

"No, of course not," said the witch. "They're normal peas again. You can't do anything with them anymore."

"You can do something with them," said the hare.

The witch looked at him questioningly.

"You can make pea soup with them."

"Yes!" exclaimed the hedgehog. "I'm hungry."

"But making pea soup takes a long time," said the owl.

"Too bad," said the hedgehog, disappointed.

"All of you, move over," said the witch. She picked up the bucket and walked to the big pot hanging over the fire. She turned the bucket upside down above the pot and mumbled something. The aroma of pea soup filled the room.

"I smell soup!"

"Me, too," said the owl. "But that's impossible . . ."

"That *is* possible," chuckled the witch. "Pea soup is easy to make with magic. And now all of you have to lend me a hand."

"With what?"

"Eating," said the witch as she set bowls out on the table.

FLOWERS FOR THE WICKED WITCH

The hare was dreaming of a deep, rumbling sound. The rumbling was so loud that he woke up.

"It wasn't a dream," he said groggily. "It really *is* rumbling outside. No, now it's gone."

He got out of bed and opened the door. He squinted into the sunlight.

"I overslept," he said in surprise. "That never happens to me. How can that be?" He thought for a moment. "I stayed up reading in bed for a long time last night . . ."

He stretched and ran outside. After a while he slowed down. "Something's wrong. But what?" He stood still and looked around.

It was very quiet in the forest. There weren't even any birds to be heard.

The hare hesitated but then started up again. It was equally empty and silent everywhere. The hare went to the hedgehog's house. The door was open, but the hedgehog wasn't home. The hare walked around the house a couple of times, then ran to the owl's tree.

"Owl?" he called anxiously.

Only the leaves rustled in the breeze.

The hare ran through the entire forest. "Owl! Hedgehog! Blackbird! Where are you?"

But nobody responded.

"Everybody's gone!" said the hare, beside himself. "Is the witch gone, too?"

He ran to the wicked witch's cabin and went inside.

The witch was sitting at the table, copying something from her book of spells.

"Thank goodness! You're still here, ma'am!" the hare exclaimed in relief. "But where are all the others?"

The witch looked up in alarm. "What are you doing here? How come you aren't gone, too?"

"What do you mean, gone?" inquired the hare. "I just woke up and . . ."

"That's why!" said the witch. "If you're asleep, the spell doesn't work, that's true."

"Spell?" asked the hare. "What spell?"

The witch pointed at her sheet of paper. "This one, here. The longest spell I've ever used. To spirit animals away."

The hare held on to the table. "Spirit away? Where have they gone, then?"

"To a remote forest," chortled the witch. "Nice and quiet."

"How mean!" cried the hare. "Conjure them back, right now!"

"No. They'll stay where they are for the time being. At least then they'll remember who's the boss here, heeheehee."

"Conjure me there, too, to that remote forest," said the hare. "All by myself I don't want to stay here."

The witch shook her head, "It's actually a good thing you're still here. That means you can help me from time to time."

The hare slammed his fist on the table. "Conjure them back or I will never look at you again!"

The witch kept on writing.

"Conjure them back! Right now!"

"No," said the witch.

"Then I'll go find them and bring them back!" said the hare and angrily walked outside.

He walked home slowly. "In which forest would they be?" he brooded. "I have to look for them, but where? I don't even know which way I have to go."

At home he prepared some bread and put it in his knapsack. "Still, I'm going to look. I don't want to stay here if the others aren't here."

He put on his knapsack and went outside. When he reached the clearing in the middle of the forest, he stood still. Which way should he go? Just straight ahead, he decided.

He was about to walk on when he heard a deep, rumbling noise. It was also getting very windy. The hare looked up.

A black cloud was headed straight for him.

"A tornado!" whispered the hare. He lay flat on the ground and shut his eyes.

The rumble grew louder. Suddenly it changed into

talking and shouting.

The hare opened his eyes.

The clearing was filled with animals. Before him sat the owl and the hedgehog, and there were the blackbird and the squirrel and the crow, the bat, the young rabbits, the birds . . .

They looked tired and dusty, but they were all back!

The hare jumped to his feet. "You're all back again!" he cried. "I was just going to look for you. Where have you been?"

"Gone," said the owl. "This morning I was just sitting by my tree, and suddenly there was this gale and then I was gone. With all the others."

"But where were you all?"

"In a dead and boring forest," said the hedgehog. "There wasn't even a pond. There was nothing to it. Bah."

All the animals shouted at the same time.

"We didn't know at all where we were . . ."

"We walked everywhere in that forest . . ."

"We were looking for the way home . . ."

"And then there was another gale . . ."

"And then we were back here again."

The owl pointed at the hare. "But where were *you*? Why weren't you in that other forest?"

"I overslept," said the hare shyly. "And if you're asleep, the spell doesn't work."

"Spell!" the hedgehog shouted triumphantly. "I told you that the wicked witch was behind it, didn't I?"

The hare nodded. "She made you disappear by

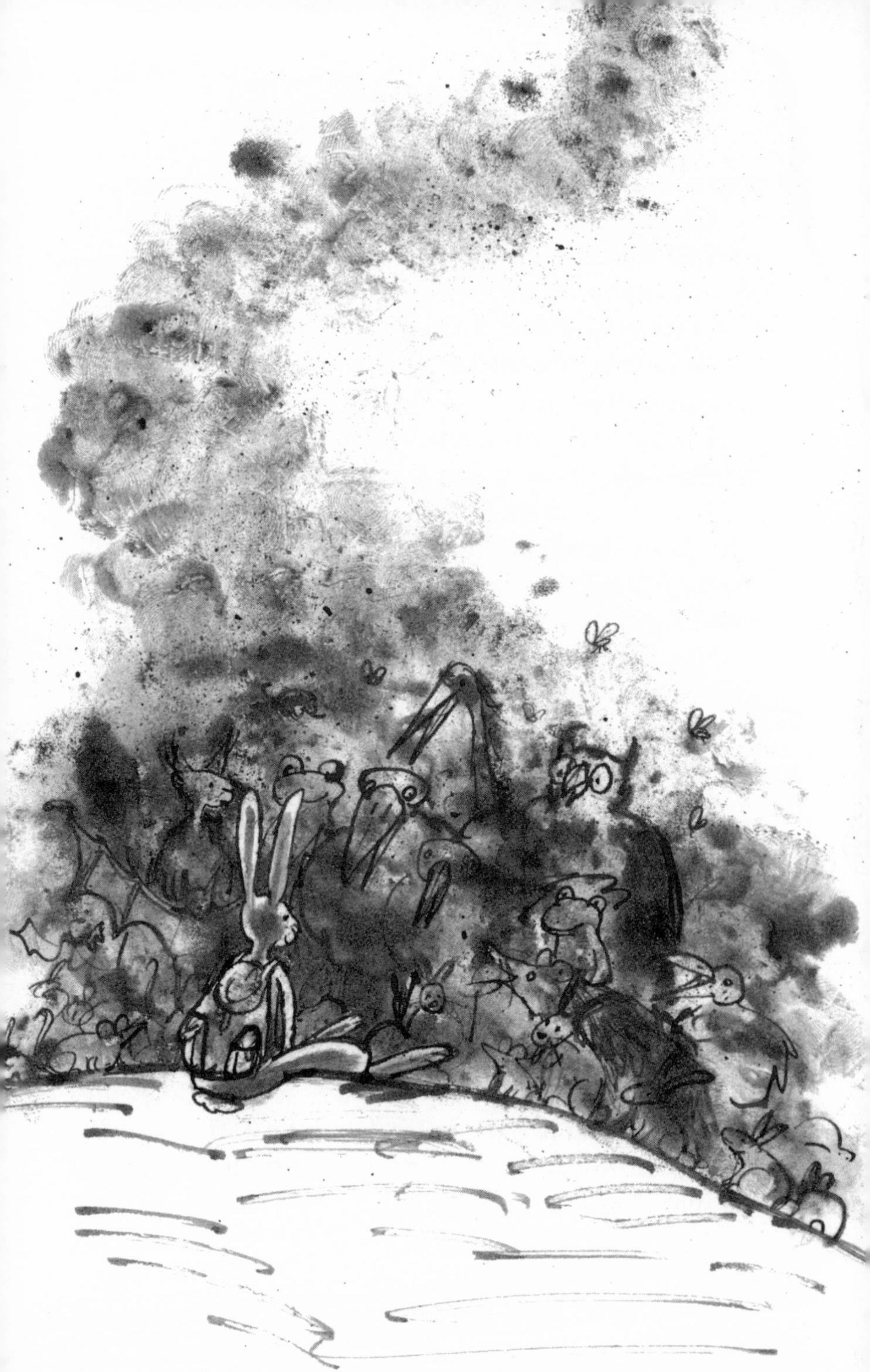

magic. With a very long spell."

"She's getting worse and worse," said the owl, shaking his head. "She didn't do things like this before."

"She didn't?" said the hedgehog. "Once she tied my spines in a knot, and . . ."

"But she's overdone things this time," said the blackbird. "Those fits of wickedness and those magic potions are bad enough. But making us disappear . . ."

The hare nodded grimly. "She has gone too far."

"We're not taking this!" shouted the crow. "Away with that woman!"

"Yes!" said the squirrel. "She has to go. Before she makes us disappear again."

"Let *her* go to that dead forest," said the hedgehog.

"Away with the witch!" the others shouted. "We're fed up with it all! Away with her! Out of our forest!"

"That's easily said," declared the blackbird. "But how do we get her to go?"

They all grew silent and looked at the hare.

"She doesn't have to go, really," said the hare. "In the end she did bring you back. But she did go too far . . ."

"And she needs to know that, too," croaked the crow. "Or else she'll do it again tomorrow."

"I won't talk to her," said the hedgehog. "That'll teach her."

"Maybe that is a good idea," said the hare pensively. "If we don't speak to her for a while, she'll understand that we're angry."

"You think so?" asked the owl.

"Yoohoo!" a shrill voice called out.

The animals looked around. "There she is," whispered the hedgehog.

The wicked witch stood at the edge of the clearing.

"Have a nice trip?" she said with a snicker. "That way you get to see something of the world at least, heeheehee."

No one said a word, no one looked at her.

The witch stopped chortling to herself. "For this once I conjured you all back. But if you give me any trouble, I'll whisk you back to the other forest in no time."

The hare turned around and walked away. The other animals stood up and followed him.

The witch was left behind, all by herself in the clearing.

A week later the hare and the owl and the hedgehog were sitting in the clearing again.

"Has either of you seen the witch lately?" asked the hare.

"No," said the owl. "At the beginning of the week I did, but then I quickly flew away."

"I saw her a couple of days ago," the hedgehog recounted. "She even said good morning. But I acted like I didn't see her."

The hare drummed on the ground. Suddenly he got up. "I'm going to see her. Are you coming?"

"To see her?" exclaimed the hedgehog. "We weren't going to have anything to do with her anymore because she went too far!"

"Yes," said the hare, "but maybe she's sick. Or sad. If you don't want to come, I'll go alone."

The owl got up. "I'll go with you."

"Me, too," said the hedgehog.

The witch's cabin looked forlorn.

"There's no smoke coming out of the chimney," said the owl.

The hare walked up to the window and looked in.

"Is she home?" asked the hedgehog.

"Yes," said the hare. "But she's packing her suitcase!"

"Her suitcase?" the owl asked uneasily.

"Then she must be going on vacation," said the hedgehog.

The hare walked over to the door and went in. "Good afternoon . . ."

The witch glanced up. She looked tired.

"Are you going on a trip?" asked the hedgehog.

"Yes," said the witch dully. "I think I'll go away."

"Where to?" asked the owl.

The witch sighed. "I don't know. Maybe to my sister's in the South, or else to the remote forest . . ."

She blinked her eyes.

"Why?" asked the hare.

"Everybody's angry with me. Nobody talks to me anymore," said the witch, sniffing. "I can't take it anymore. That's why I think I'll go away."

"But that—that isn't necessary at all," the hare said, stumbling over his words.

"We stopped being angry a long time ago," said the owl.

"You can just stay here," said the hedgehog.

The witch put her book of magic spells into the suitcase. "No. It's better if I go away."

The hare drummed on the table.

The owl plucked at his feathers.

The hedgehog stared at the suitcase.

Suddenly the hare bounded toward the door. "Don't leave yet!" he called. "Wait a minute until we're back."

He pulled the others outside with him.

"She's really going," said the owl, upset. "For good."

"She's leaving us alone," said the hedgehog in a little voice.

"Now we've gone too far," said the hare. "The poor woman . . ."

"We have to keep her from going," said the owl breathlessly.

"But how?"

"We'll all push on the door!" cried the hedgehog. "Then she can't get out."

"That won't help," said the hare. "She has to know that we really aren't angry at her anymore."

He thought deeply.

"Owl, we're going to get the others. Hedgehog, you go pick flowers. As many as possible. Hurry! We don't have much time."

The witch closed her suitcase and looked around. She looked at the cupboard full of little jars and bottles, at her witch's cauldron; she ran her hand over her chair. Then she heaved a deep sigh.

She lifted the suitcase off the table, took her broom from the corner, and slowly walked toward the door.

But all of a sudden the door flew open and there were the hare and the hedgehog, with flowers. The hedgehog pointed at the suitcase. "You were going to wait!" he cried. "You promised!"

"Yes," said the witch. "But . . ."

"Luckily we're just in time," said the hare. "Here, these flowers are for you, madam."

The witch put down her suitcase and her broom and accepted the flowers. "But I can't take them with me, can I?"

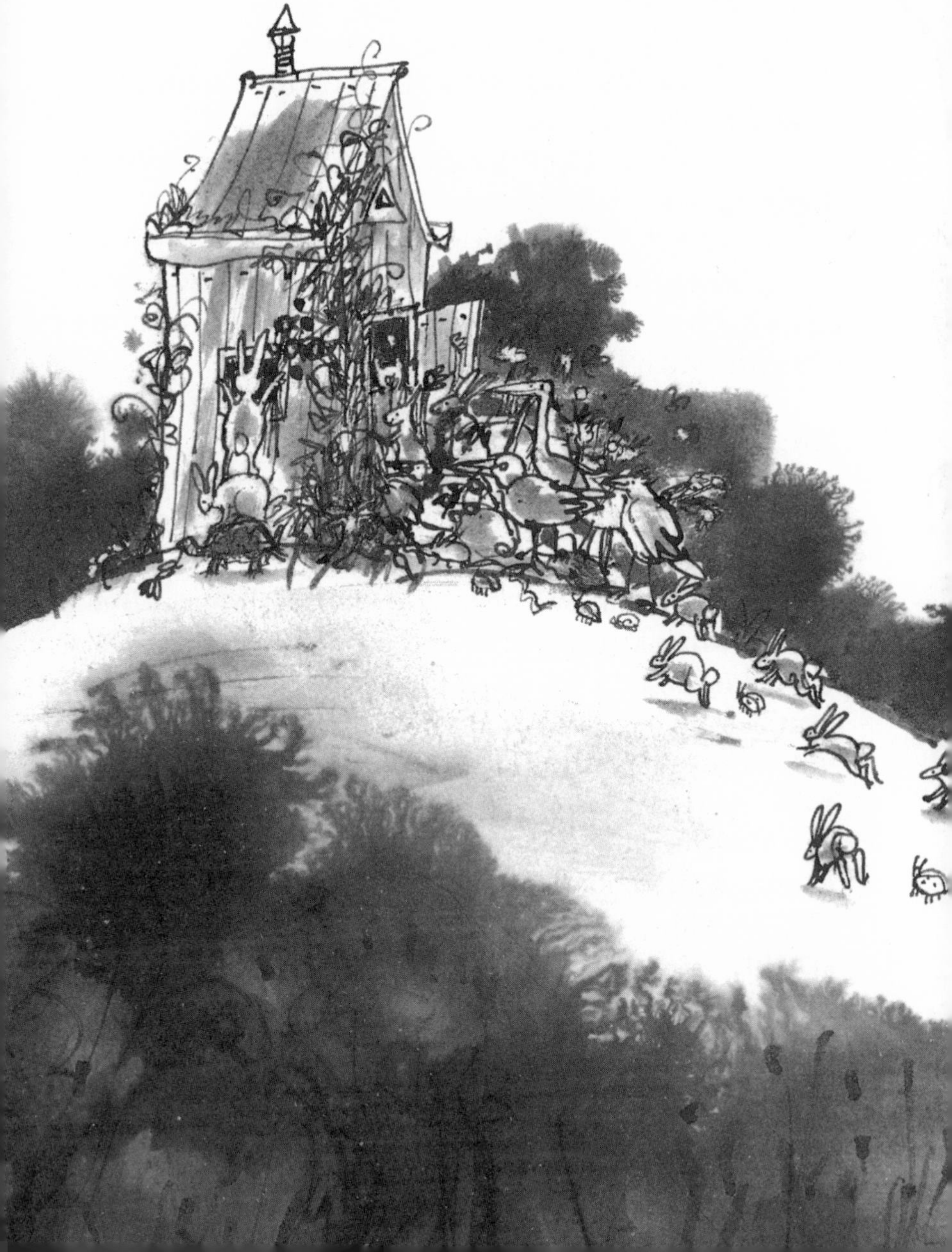

The owl and the blackbird came in, also carrying flowers. "For you," said the owl. "And we hope that you'll stay for a long time to come, madam."

"Stay?" asked the witch. "But . . ."

The young rabbits hopped inside and shoved and elbowed one another aside. "Look, Witch! Look at the pretty flowers! All for you!"

The squirrel and the crow stood in the doorway holding flowers.

The witch looked out. All the animals of the forest were standing in front of her door and they had all brought flowers.

The witch wiped her eyes.

"Don't cry," said the hedgehog, feeling uncomfortable. "I can't bear that at all."

The hare jumped up on a chair. "In short," he said solemnly, "madam, do you want to stay with us?"

"Please?" wheedled the hedgehog.

The witch blew her nose with a honk. "But I thought that you all wanted me gone."

"We thought so, too," the hare said quickly. "But you belong here, ma'am, with us."

"A forest without a witch, that's not right, is it?" said the owl.

The witch pushed her suitcase under the table. "I'm staying," she said, beaming.

"Hurrah!" all the animals cheered. "Long live our witch!"

"And from now on, no more magic!" cried the blackbird.

The witch's face clouded over. "That's impossible," she said. "I happen to be a witch, and a witch simply has to do magic."

The hare smiled. "The blackbird means that you mustn't make us disappear anymore. But those other spells and those magic potions of yours, ma'am, we can handle those."

"Sure we can!" exclaimed the hedgehog. "Do as much magic as you want."

"I'll conjure up some soup," said the witch. "For all of us."

She mumbled a spell. It began to smell delicious in the witch's cabin, and the cauldron in the corner was suddenly full of steaming soup.

"Soup for everybody!" said the witch. "And if there isn't enough, I'll simply conjure up some more."

The hedgehog gave the blackbird a nudge. "Now you see how handy that magic of hers is? A witch in the forest, that's practical."